A Vineyard Love

The Vineyard Sunset Series

Katie Winters

ALL RIGHTS RESERVED. No part of this publication may be reproduced, distributed, or transmitted in any form or by any means, including photocopying, recording, or other electronic or mechanical methods, without the prior written permission of the publisher.

Copyright © 2023 by Katie Winters

This is a work of fiction. Any resemblance of characters to actual persons, living or dead is purely coincidental. Katie Winters holds exclusive rights to this work. Unauthorized duplication is prohibited.

Chapter One

It was Amanda Harris' wedding day, and so far, everything had gone exactly as she'd planned.

This would have been a blessing for any bride, but for Amanda, who, two and a half years ago, had tried to marry Chris in a "perfect wedding" that had ended in him leaving her at the altar, it was a Godsend. When all that had happened, Amanda had been crushed and had moved to Martha's Vineyard from Newark to nurse her wounds near the comforts of her mother, Susan, and her cousin, Audrey. But not long after Chris had left her, Amanda had miraculously met someone else. "Life is what happens when you're busy making other plans," John Lennon had said. He'd been right.

"Remember how everyone else knew you were in love with Sam before you did?" Amanda's cousin and dearest friend, Audrey, stood beside Amanda in the glorious and ornate foyer of the Aquinnah Cliffside Overlook Hotel, which had only opened one week ago, smiling at her and gripping her bouquet of peonies nervously. It was five minutes before the double-wide doors would open out onto the beautiful stretch of green field that lined the cliffs. Between lines of white chairs situated on the lush green, Susan would walk Amanda toward the love of her life and the rest of their days together. "You were so resistant to the idea of falling in love with him at first," Audrey remembered. "But all anyone could do was talk about the way you looked at him."

Amanda's cheeks burned at the memory of those first few months when Sam had known intuitively to take things slowly. He'd sensed that Amanda had been damaged beyond belief and was unwilling to leap into romance too quickly. She'd had to be sure he was the one.

"We've already been through so much together," Amanda breathed, eyeing her reflection in the floor-to-ceiling mirror in the foyer, which presented a blushing bride, her hair gleaming, half-up and half-down, just the way she'd requested it.

"Gosh, yes. Thinking back over the past few years makes my head spin. There were babies, weddings, car accidents, romances, sailing trips, and mysterious newcomers to the island. Oh, and never forget, we helped Mom direct that play and got snowed in during the blizzard of winter '22. Remember?" As Amanda spun with the list of memories, Audrey paused, her eyes focused on the crowd outside. "It's going to be hard to wrap my mind around you leaving the Sheridan House for good, though. Max will not know what to do with himself without his Aunt Amanda around. And Grandpa and I will probably spend our days eating cookies and cereal."

Amanda chuckled. "Noah will be moving in soon. Maybe he can make a salad every now and again?" She was referring to Audrey's fiancé, who'd made the decision

A Vineyard Love

to move into the Sheridan House in the wake of Amanda's departure. Everything was changing.

"Are you kidding? He's worse than we are," Audrey said.

Out on the field, Amanda's two hundred guests listened to the five-string quintet play "Pachelbel's Canon" as they settled into their white chairs. Most everyone had arrived an hour and a half ago for pre-wedding cocktails and snacks, swapping stories and compliments as time ticked toward the wedding. In the suite they'd rented for the bride to prepare, Amanda had felt like a celebrity who couldn't go downstairs for fear of the paparazzi. Still, she'd made sure the staff had brought cocktails and snacks up to her, Audrey, Susan, Lola, Christine, and Amanda's two best friends from Newark, Brittany and Brooke. Together, they'd spent the vast majority of the previous few hours laughing, crying, and getting their hair and makeup done. Such was the life of a Sheridan woman— awash with every emotion, yet never one to refuse a meal.

Susan, Amanda's gorgeous mother, wore a periwinkle dress, her hair cascading in gorgeous curls along her shoulder. At forty-seven, the mother of two and grand-mother of three was powerful and sleek, a well-known defense lawyer who'd also battled breast cancer and won. Her return to the island three years ago, when Grandpa Wesley had been diagnosed with dementia, had brought everyone else home to mend the wounds from the past. Everyone agreed that Susan Sheridan was the matriarch of the family, their central heartbeat. Amanda loved her more than words. In fact, growing up, she'd wanted to be her mother, so much so that she'd forced her brother to "play" lawyer in the living room of the old house in Newark.

"How are you feeling, honey?" Susan smiled and swept a few rogue strands of hair behind Amanda's shoulder.

"Like I might faint," Amanda said with a laugh. "But otherwise, good."

"I don't think you have anything to worry about," Susan assured her, glancing back toward Christine and Lola, both of whom wore beautiful periwinkle dresses and clung to similar bouquets. At forty-four and forty-one, respectively, Christine and Lola were Susan's beloved little sisters, both of whom had found love on the island in the years since their return.

"Everything is exactly as you planned it," Lola said. "This is Amanda Harris we're talking about. She gets what she wants."

Amanda laughed, her eyes flitting around nervously. It took everything within her not to point out that last time, that wasn't true— that her fiancé had done everything in his power to flee the ceremony and leave her to explain the circumstances to her guests. *But what could she possibly say to explain something like that?* Everyone had understood that he just hadn't loved her enough. It was just that simple.

Suddenly, a figure appeared in front of the double-wide doors that led out onto the lush green grass. He wrestled the doorknob until Lola rushed to open it.

"Noah?" Audrey laughed at the sight of her fiancé, who looked stricken, his face pale. "Noah, did you really not find them yet?"

Amanda's stomach clenched. "Find what?"

Audrey waved her hand as Noah approached,

limping forward like a zombie. Amanda let her bouquet hand fall to her side. Within Noah's eyes, she saw something very sinister.

"Find what?" Amanda demanded again when nobody else said anything.

Audrey placed her hand around Noah's arm. "Baby, what's going on?"

Noah raised his eyes to Amanda. He looked like a student who'd been caught doing something very wrong and now had to confess it in front of the entire class. "The rings are missing," he explained timidly.

Amanda closed her eyes, feeling the world spin around her. "It's okay," she heard herself stutter. "We can just fake it and find them later." She and Sam had gone out of their way to select the perfect rings for the ceremony, but now they'd have to improvise until after the wedding. It was disappointing, but it wasn't the end of the world.

But when she opened her eyes, Noah took another soft step toward her. It was clear he wasn't done yet.

"Noah? What else?" Amanda's voice jumped nervously.

"Noah, you can't be so cagey right now," Susan warned him. "We have two hundred guests out there, ready for the wedding in just a couple of minutes."

"I can't find Sam, either," Noah finished.

Amanda frowned. "What did you just say?"

Audrey leaped toward Amanda, her eyes panicked. "I'm sure he's somewhere around here. He wouldn't do this. I mean, come on. It's Sam!"

But Amanda's head had already begun to twist, her thoughts contorting. Slowly, she backed into the wall behind her and dropped her head against it. She was no longer completely focused on what people said in front of her, nor their opinions. She was now back in the nightmare of January 2021, when she'd learned she wasn't worthy of love.

"Did you look back in the suite where you were getting ready?" Susan demanded of Noah, speaking to him like she was in the courtroom.

"Of course. But that's where I was when we first lost him!"

Susan's hand was in a fist. "Charlotte? Where's Charlotte?" She scanned the foyer, then ducked into the adjacent hallway to find the wedding planner, Susan's cousin, who wore a headset and smiled happily. "Charlotte, we have a situation. We can't find the groom."

Charlotte's smile fell off her face. "I'm on it," she said, disappearing through the double-wide doors and out across the green.

Audrey spoke to Amanda, trying to console her, but Amanda only got bits and pieces of it. She'd heard *Sam wouldn't do this to you,* and *he loves you,* but what Audrey didn't understand was that, once upon a time, Amanda never would have imagined Chris would have done that, either.

"Maybe it was all a game to him," Amanda said very quietly. "Maybe he wanted to make me fall in love with him, just to do this to me again?"

"No!" Audrey protested. "He's got to be around here somewhere."

But that moment, Charlotte burst back into the foyer with more news. "Have you seen Kelli?"

Their cousin, Kelli Montgomery, was the hotel manager of the Aquinnah Cliffside Overlook Hotel. Two summers ago, she'd been instrumental in its purchase by a man named Xander Van Tress, and together, they'd built it back to its former glory and beyond. They'd also fallen in love along the way.

"She said she was going to be here," Susan muttered. "She wouldn't miss Amanda's wedding."

"There's been a lot of chaos at the hotel today," Noah mentioned, his eyes flashing. "She probably had to take care of something."

"That's no reason to miss a family wedding," Susan said.

A moment later, Sam's younger brother, Xavier , appeared in the foyer, similarly panicked. "Have you seen Sam?"

Amanda crumpled into herself against the wall, rolling in and out of fits of panic. As everyone before her spoke all over one another, spitting questions and offering solutions to find her groom, Amanda began to face her fate: Sam had probably left her at the altar. And she was going to have to start a brand-new life all over again.

Chapter Two

One Week Earlier

Kelli awoke at sunrise. It was Saturday, opening day of the Aquinnah Cliffside Overlook Hotel, the first day of the rest of her life, and she couldn't waste any time. Leaving the handsome Xander Van Tress in bed, his muscular arm wrapped tenderly around the glowing sheets, she tip-toed to the bathroom to shower and do her makeup and hair. As she slid into a two-piece suit and adjusted the jacket over her shoulders, she knowingly eyed herself in the mirror and said, "Come on, Kelli Montgomery. You've been preparing for this for nearly two years. You can do this." Still, Kelli felt jittery with doubt.

Downstairs, Xander was up, brewing a pot of coffee and scraping peanut butter over a slice of toast he said she was legally required to eat. He kissed her dutifully on the cheek, careful not to mess up her lipstick, then whispered, "But we'll do plenty of kissing when we get home tonight."

Kelli's cheeks were warm. "You're still coming up today, aren't you?"

"Of course! I'll be there by eight," Xander affirmed.

"And you have the list of to-dos I gave you?"

"I put the list in my phone so I wouldn't lose track of it," Xander told her.

As Kelli sipped her coffee, a text buzzed through on her phone. It was from Susan Sheridan, her cousin, whom Kelli both loved and felt equally annoyed at.

> SUSAN: Good luck today with the opening!
>
> SUSAN: I'm so relieved you managed to open in time for Amanda's wedding next week.
>
> SUSAN: That was touch and go!

Kelli grimaced and decided to text Susan back later. As the construction and design crew had restructured the old Aquinnah Cliffside Overlook Hotel for the past two years, Kelli's brain had been twisted with worries that had only doubled in size when Susan had set the date for her daughter's wedding to June 10. Last autumn, Kelli had been sure the redesign would be finished by then. But as time had gone on, it had become increasingly clear just how complicated a redesign of this nature was— and they'd just-barely managed to open one week before Amanda's wedding.

"Was that Susan?" Xander could read Kelli like a book.

"She's a nervous wreck. I get that." Kelli tried to laugh it off. "But I have two hundred guests staying at my new luxury hotel tonight, and I have to somehow throw them a party, keep them safe, and ensure they write amazing Google reviews, all for the future of my employment. I can't think about Susan's anxiety right now!"

"Then don't." Xander said things like this simply, as though choosing what you thought about was easy.

"Are you really such a master of your own emotions?" Kelli collected her car keys and glanced at herself in the mirror.

"You're going to be great, Kelli." Xander gave her a soulful look that told her he meant business. "You and that old hotel are the two greatest things that ever happened to me. I can't wait to see what happens next."

As Kelli drove through the gorgeous June morning en route to the Aquinnah Cliffside Overlook Hotel, she could only think back over the previous two years. Back then, she'd been newly separated from Mike, her verbally abusive ex-husband, and had been working as a real estate agent, just like her parents before her. Kerry and Trevor Montgomery had always spoken about the Aquinnah Cliffside Overlook Hotel, which had been destroyed during a hurricane in the forties. Nobody in the family had completely understood the dramatic history that had linked their family to the old place, until Kelli had learned so much more when she'd tried to sell it to the handsome developer, Xander Van Tress, who always purchased old, romantic properties.

What had happened was back in the forties, the luxurious and elegant Aquinnah Cliffside Overlook Hotel had been owned by Robert Sheridan, Kelli's grandfather. During a particularly strange summer, a very rich man named James arrived on the island with his wife, Marilyn, who would eventually become Kelli's grandmother. James had come to the island to buy the hotel from Robert, but she wanted to believe her so badly. "How do you like the island so far?"

"It's beautiful! I don't know if I've ever been to a place like this before. Back in Providence, things got bad for me," Sandra said. "I wasn't sure how the rest of my life was going to go. But here, I've already met some wonderful friends, and I feel very positive. Maybe that's naive?"

"No," Kelli assured her. "I think positivity is a wonderful tool that we can use to build better futures. I tell myself that, anyway."

As luck would have it, Kelli had a spare set of flats in the office. When the swelling of her ankle went down a bit, she slid her feet into the flats and showed them off to Sandra, who clapped and said, "It's already evening, which means most people have had one too many cocktails to notice you changed your shoes."

Kelli laughed. "You're probably right. Besides, people come to an event like this to be seen. They don't care about what the hotel manager looks like, right?"

"Absolutely," Sandra said, opening the office door for Kelli, who strode out— acting, yet again, like she owned the place. She basically did.

Kelli and Sandra re-entered the ballroom, where the dining room tables had been set for a five-course meal. Still, the guests mingled, showing off their expensive dresses and their tans, which they'd gotten from Mediterranean vacations, or trips to the Bahamas. Kelli had never been one to take such lavish off-island vacations, as she liked to take every season on Martha's Vineyard as it came.

"Sandra?" A voice came from somewhere in the

Robert seemed inconvincible, keeping Robert and Marilyn at the hotel longer. James hadn't known that his wife, Marilyn, and Robert had fallen in love at first sight and begun an exhilarating affair. Around the time James learned about the affair, Robert sold the rights of the hotel over to him— only a few hours before the hotel itself crumbled beneath tremendous hurricane winds and rain. James had granted Marilyn a divorce and fled the island, taking his ownership papers of the hotel along with him.

Two summers ago, Kelli and Xander had tracked down James' son, who'd explained the story and eventually passed over the rights of the hotel to Kelli and Xander, who'd decided to keep it in the family. By then, Kelli and Xander had fallen in love, anyway.

Kelli parked her car outside of the hotel and gazed up at it, coffee in hand. The construction crew had done a remarkable job of upholding the luxurious spirit of the old place while adding artistic touches here and there that made it something else, something uniquely Kelli and Xander's. Kelli had begun to think of her and Xander's love in a similar vein to Marilyn and Robert's. It was their second chance, their leap into the ether even after so many other things in life had told them not to hope. They weren't naive this time, but they were happy and knew how to generate that happiness from nothingness.

Kelli stepped through the double-wide doors of the old and beautiful place, then paused in the foyer to take stock of the artistic design that she had had a hand in creating. On the wall hung several gorgeous paintings of Martha's Vineyard throughout history: violent storms above sailboats, gorgeous purple fogs around lighthouses, and the jagged cliffs just outside. Each of the paintings had been commissioned by local artists and had cost the hotel an arm and a leg. Seeing them hanging along the beautiful walls, Kelli felt it was worth it.

"Morning, ma'am!" One of the front desk workers, Piper, whipped past with a smile, carrying a box of supplies. "We're almost set up at the front desk."

"That's fantastic, Piper." Kelli jumped to action, walking past the front desk, through the beautiful combination dining room and ballroom, which had been designed to imitate the old ballroom, then up a back staircase toward her private office. There, Kelli fetched her itinerary, gave herself another pep talk, then returned to the foyer to welcome the fifty-seven members of staff who would be at the hotel over the next week of their "soft" open. Kelli wasn't sure exactly why this opening was so "soft." It felt ridiculously heavy, the sort of thing that would destroy her if she didn't keep her wits about her.

As Kelli stood in the foyer, her staff members gathered and peered at her with a mix of excitement and intrigue. There was joy in being a part of the very first group of employees at a brand-new place. It was up to them to create the magic.

"Good morning!" Kelli began, grateful that her voice sounded confident. "Welcome to your very first day at the Aquinnah Cliffside Overlook Hotel. I've hired all of you because I believe you have the singular power to make this place just as elegant as it once was, all those years ago when my grandfather walked these halls."

Kelli half-blacked-out during her pep talk, congratulating the people before her, their work ethic, and their drive. "The first guests will begin to check in by one. The bar needs to be open and prepped by then, as many guests will want afternoon wine and cocktails after their journey to the Vineyard. Chef Billiard, I assume you're prepping for lunch?"

Kelli spoke eloquently with her staff, nodding as they explained their plan, as though she hadn't already pestered them to give her that information before. Nothing could be left to chance. Everything had to be perfect.

By two-thirty that afternoon, the Aquinnah Cliffside Overlook Hotel was swarming with guests. They were well-dressed, often wearing white or cream linen, holding cocktails, and laughing with one another as the late spring sunlight dove through the windows and glinted across the tiled floors of the foyer and the hardwood of the ballroom. Another fifty or so guests were outside, seated beneath umbrellas and taking in the view of the glorious cliffs along the edge of the lush green grass. In only a week, Amanda Harris' wedding would be set up right here, presenting the newlyweds with a remarkable view of the glittering horizon.

"There she is!" Suddenly, Kelli's father was before her, smiling gently. He had a cocktail in hand and waved toward Kelli's mother, saying, "I found her! You've been difficult to track down, you know."

"I have to be everywhere at once," Kelli explained, hugging her father, then her mother.

"Darling, we're just so proud of you," Kerry said. "My father would have been over the moon to see the old place up and running."

Kelli took a small moment to really feel what her mother told her, then said, "I hate how stressed I am. I wish I could enjoy it."

Trevor gestured toward a long table a bit further through the crowd, where all of Kelli's Sheridan cousins and Montgomery siblings sat, enjoying one another's company. When Kelli spotted them, they all waved. Even Kelli's children, Lexie, Sam, and Josh, sat at the table, their smiles enormous. Kelli hurried over to them and hugged them as though she hadn't seen them in years. Because she would always be their mother, she demanded if they'd had enough to eat and if they were drinking enough water between glasses of wine. They rolled their eyes and shooed her away, saying, "You have work to do!"

It was four-thirty, and Kelli already felt like she'd walked one thousand miles in her heels. Perhaps it had been a mistake to wear them, but then again, they gave her the kind of confidence she felt she needed in front of so many guests and employees. She took a moment in the foyer when she thought nobody was watching to close her eyes and take a deep breath. Just her luck, Xander entered the foyer, tracking her down again.

"There she is. The woman of the hour."

Kelli laughed and opened her eyes.

"Were you napping?"

Kelli swatted him. "I was just thinking about how nice it will be to take off these shoes sometime in the next ten hours."

Xander winced. "That bad?"

"I'm just exhausted, and it's only day one," Kelli said.

"It'll get easier," Xander assured her. "And like I said, I think you need to hire someone to pick up some of the slack."

Kelli hesitated. She'd assumed she could juggle everything herself, the way she'd watched Susan Sheridan juggle motherhood, cancer, new love, and a new law office, seemingly with ease.

"Don't be a hero," Xander said. "But hey! I have to run. I have to put out a fire myself."

"Don't even tell me what it is," Kelli begged him. "I can only deal with so much drama at once."

"I'll keep it to myself," Xander assured her, then sped off.

Kelli sighed, then got up the nerve to walk back toward the party. But just before she turned the corner to enter the ballroom, something incredible happened. The heel of her right shoe snapped beneath her, and her ankle went sideways toward the ground. Kelli tumbled, just out of sight of her guests, and sat on the ground, at a loss, staring at her ankle, which would surely bruise.

What was she going to do?

Chapter Three

Just as Kelli made peace with the idea of clambering back to her feet and limping to her office to hide from her guests for the rest of the day, a twenty-something staff member spotted her and hurried over. "Oh my gosh! Kelli, are you all right?"

Kelli winced as she looked up at the young woman, who dropped to inspect her ankle. The woman had mousy brown hair but intelligent eyes, and she wore an outfit that indicated she was a bellhop, someone who carried luggage to people's rooms. Kelli didn't recognize her; the head bellhop had probably hired her instead of Kelli.

"My heel broke," Kelli explained timidly. "I feel very stupid right now."

The woman raised her chin to lock her gaze with Kelli's. "Don't feel stupid. Can you put pressure on it?"

Kelli said she thought she probably could, but she allowed the young woman to help her to her feet, where she learned her ankle was definitely messed up and needed a bit of ice. Slowly, they went through the kitchen to retrieve ice and up the back to get to Kelli's office, where the young woman wrapped the ice in a towel and placed it tenderly on Kelli's ankle.

"Wow," Kelli said. "What would I have done without you?"

"Don't worry about it! I saw you on the ground, and my instincts took over. I was a lifeguard when I was younger."

Kelli smiled at the young woman, who spoke a little too quickly, as though she was constantly nervous. "What's your name?"

"I'm Sandra," the woman said.

"Nice to meet you, Sandra. I'm Kelli. I take it you work as a bellhop?"

Sandra said she did. "It's my first job on the island," Sandra went on. "I just got here about a month ago and read about the new hotel opening by the cliffs. Since I needed a job, I jumped for it and was so relieved when Greg called me and said I was in."

Kelli felt at ease for the first time all day, chatting with this young woman who adored her job so much, who was just so grateful to be there. "Have you ever worked in hospitality before?"

"Never," Sandra said, "although I told Greg that I had. Please, don't tell him."

Kelli laughed. "I've never really worked in hospitality, either. I took a six-week course on hotel management last year, but I don't think you can learn anything like this through a course. It has to be hands-on."

"It seems like you're doing a really good job so far," Sandra said. "I mean, everyone respects you and listens to you."

Kelli wasn't sure if the young woman was lying, but

crowd. Kelli watched as Amanda burst out, waving at Sandra. "I had no idea you would be here!"

Kelli eyed Amanda curiously as she flung her arms around Sandra, her engagement ring glinting.

"That job I was telling you about was here!" Sandra said as the hug broke.

"Wow. You should have told me! Kelli and I are related," Amanda said. "In fact, I'm having my wedding right here next week."

"Same time, same place," Kelli said, wavering with nerves.

"What a wonderful location for a wedding," Sandra said.

"How do you two know each other?" Kelli asked.

"Sandra and I met at yoga class," Amanda explained. "Probably about a month ago, now, right?"

"I started going when I arrived," Sandra explained.

"That's right. Sandra's a brand-new islander! But I think we already have you wrapped around our fingers," Amanda teased. "You won't know how to leave after a summer here."

Amanda then turned back to Kelli and touched her elbow delicately. "How are you holding up, Kelli?"

Kelli lied through her teeth. "Everything is going perfectly. I'm over the moon!"

"Everything has been divine so far," Amanda said, just as her fiancé, Sam, approached, placed his hand on Amanda's lower back, and beamed at Kelli.

"This place is spectacular," Sam said. "And the staff are superb."

"If you like it so much, maybe I'll steal you away from the Sunrise Cove to help out," Kelli teased.

"I don't know about that. Even after just two years, the Sunrise Cove has my heart," Sam said.

Sam worked as the hotel manager at the Sunrise Cove Inn because everyone else in the Sheridan family had separate projects and couldn't work at the inn full-time. Now that he was marrying Amanda, the hotel would again be a family-run business— yet another generation, seeing the inn through tourist season after tourist season.

"Why don't you come over and have a drink with us?" Amanda urged Kelli.

Kelli's head rang with the thoughts of everything she still had to do, everything she still had to check up on.

"You have time," Sandra told her quietly. "Dinner starts in an hour, at which time you can do everything else you need to do."

Kelli tilted her head, wondering how the young woman had read her thoughts so clearly. "Well, all right. Just one drink."

Sandra smiled and tapped her nose. "I have to run. I'll see you later, Amanda. Maybe even at yoga on Monday?"

"I wouldn't miss it," Amanda said as she guided Kelli back through the crowd.

Familiar, smiling faces called out to Kelli as she approached. First, her little brother, Andy, burst up to hug her, overwhelming her with his excitement.

"I can't believe this place, Kelli," he said.

"You built some of the furniture in here! You were such a help in bringing the old magic to life," Kelli reminded him.

Andy blushed and palmed his neck. "Sure. Yeah. But we delivered that furniture a few months back, and it feels like the whole place has changed since then."

"Oh, Kelli." Kelli's younger sisters, Charlotte and

A Vineyard Love

Claire, hurried forward to hug Kelli, their eyes alight. Charlotte and Claire had always been the best of friends, and now, even their careers aligned— one a florist and the other a wedding planner. Unfortunately for the Martha's Vineyard families, now that Charlotte's daughter was off to college in the fall, Charlotte had agreed to move to Orcas Island with Everett, her fiancé, who'd taken a job as a travel writer on that island all the way across the continent.

And finally, behind her sisters came the stoic face of her elder brother, Steve, who, as it turned out, had a plus one. "Kelli, it really is something special," he said as he hugged her. "I hope you don't mind that I brought a friend?"

"Rita!" Kelli greeted the woman with the short, black bob with a genuine smile and a hug. "It's good to see you again. Are you back from California for long?"

"Just a week," Rita explained. "Steve invited me to the wedding, and I was lucky enough to finish out a project back home and hit the road."

"What project was it?" Charlotte asked, her voice lowering.

"Yeah! Give us the gossip," Claire said.

Rita laughed, accustomed to everyone's obsession with her career as a private detective. "I was looking for someone's ex-husband. He'd disappeared without a trace, or so his ex-wife had thought. Fortunately, it took just a brief scan through his phone records to realize he'd moved to Las Vegas to be with his mistress, where he'd already lost hundreds of thousands of dollars of his children's college funds."

"My gosh!" Kelli's eyes widened.

Beside Rita, Steve smiled, impressed with his new

friend. Steve had met Rita during a very strange spring, during which Rita had come to the island to investigate a missing young woman. And it just so happened that Steve and his daughter, Isabella, had helped Rita crack the case — and everyone was pretty sure Rita and Steve had found a little love along the way. But because Steve had only just lost his wife last autumn, Steve wanted to bide his time. Everyone understood that, too.

Isabella could be seen behind Steve, together with her new boyfriend, Rhett, who'd been released from the hospital looking handsome and healthy. Isabella tossed her head with laughter at something Rhett said, and Kelli's heart ballooned with gladness.

"This is what I wanted the hotel to be," Kelli heard herself say.

"What do you mean?" Steve asked.

Kelli chuckled, feeling embarrassed. "I wanted it to be a place of love, celebration, and joy."

"I think you've achieved that to a T," Steve said. "I haven't seen a single person here not having an iconic time. You did that, Kell. Remember that."

She eventually tore herself from her family to tend to other obligations. During that time, the guests sat for a five-course meal of honey-glazed leg of lamb with mustard and thyme, roasted potatoes, mini beef tourtieres, baked brie with figs, and a lemon dessert, all of which Kelli knew was to die for as she and Xander had sampled the menu a few days ago to prepare.

"There she is!" Xander's voice came from deep down the hallway, and although she was speeding off to check on the kitchen staff, Kelli turned and allowed herself to collapse in his arms. Xander kissed her forehead and said, "How are you feeling, my love?"

"Like a wilted leaf."

"But a happy wilted leaf?"

"The happiest." Kelli raised her chin to smile at him, both overwhelmed and overjoyed.

"This was our dream, Kelli," Xander reminded her, drawing her hand into his and placing his opposite hand on her lower back. Like a sailboat, he rocked her, there in the foyer, slowly dancing to the music that streamed in from the ballroom. "Promise me that you'll take a moment to appreciate it every now and again."

"I know. You're right." Kelli laughed at herself, at her fears and her worries. "Thank you for being a part of my dream."

"Tonight, I'm going to massage your feet," Xander teased her. "And make you a big cup of hot cocoa and let you watch whatever TV show you want."

"Wow. You really are Mr. Romance, aren't you?" Kelli laughed and kissed him again, listening as the crowd in the ballroom gossiped and sipped their glasses of champagne and celebrated the lemon cake, which was moist and delectable, an old family recipe that Chef Billiard had sworn he would never tell anyone, not on his life.

Chapter Four

It was just past midnight when the party began to die out. Amanda, who'd quit drinking hours ago in order to drive herself and Sam back home, retreated from the ballroom to the nearest bathroom to re-apply her lipstick. Once there, none other than Audrey bolted from the bathroom stall, smiling sleepily and happily.

"My gosh! Look at you! You're one week away from marrying Sam!"

Amanda blushed and adjusted her dress, a navy-blue number that showed a little more skin than she was used to. "It's weird," Amanda confessed now. "I used to think twenty-five was so old. I figured I'd already be two years into marriage by now, with at least one baby."

Audrey wrinkled her nose. "If twenty-five is old, what's forty-five? And if you're planning on telling Lola Sheridan she's old, give me a heads-up so I can clear the area. Besides, I had my baby when I was nineteen! I wouldn't wish that drama on anyone. You've been allowed to enjoy your twenties, make mistakes, and fall in love all over again with a really great guy. Who wouldn't want that?"

Amanda and Audrey returned to the party, where Noah and Sam held glasses of whiskey and chatted near the fireplace, which now roared, given the lateness of the hour and the chill in the air. Since Audrey had met Noah in the NICU ward at the hospital after Max's birth, the two had been inseparable, which had, in turn, led Sam and Noah to become very dear friends. Now that Noah and Audrey were also engaged, it seemed that they were headed for decades of Christmases, sailing adventures, and family picnics.

"There she is!" Sam turned to Amanda, tugged her closer to him, and kissed her on the cheek. "Would you like to step outside with me for a moment?"

Amanda was delirious when it came to Sam. She could do nothing but say yes to him. She linked her fingers with his and allowed him to guide her outside, where a smattering of stars blanketed the inky black sky above them. Below the cliffs, the Atlantic surged against the rocks. And because it was so dark, especially as they neared the cliffs' edge, it was easy to pretend they were in the middle of nowhere, miles from civilization.

"It's a dream out here," Amanda breathed.

Sam kissed her, closing his eyes as he held her close. Amanda could feel the strength of his heartbeat behind his ribcage and the promise in his touch. All she wanted was this.

"Can you believe our lives, Amanda? I mean, can you believe how lucky we are?"

Amanda shook her head. "Sometimes I can't."

He laughed that open, genuine laugh of his, then said, "Me neither."

Amanda shivered against him, raised her chin, and said, "You'd better show up on our wedding day. I mean, if you have cold feet at all, you need to tell me right now." Amanda's tone was light and cheerful, but it meant business, as well.

"Amanda!" Sam tightened his grip. His eyes glinted with understanding. He knew more than anyone how devastated Amanda had been when her ex left her at the altar. It had been one of the single most important moments in her life— and it had nearly destroyed her.

"Amanda, I wouldn't do that to you," Sam said tenderly. "All I've wanted since I met you was to marry you."

Amanda's smile widened. "That can't be true."

"It is. I swear."

"I'm sure there were at least five minutes between us meeting and you knowing you wanted to marry me," Amanda teased.

"Not five minutes. No way. It was immediate."

Amanda tossed her head back, so grateful for Sam's playfulness. Chris hadn't been funny in the slightest. They'd spent so many nights in their Newark apartment saying nothing at all. What if she'd lived like that forever?

Back in the Aquinnah Cliffside Overlook, Amanda and Sam made the rounds to say goodbye. As usual, Grandpa Wes and Beatrice were thick as thieves, dancing themselves deep into the night as though they weren't in their seventies, as though Grandpa Wes didn't have dementia, and with all the optimism of youth. Amanda hugged her grandfather, who said, "Mandy, I can't wait till next week! It's going to be spectacular."

Afterward, Amanda tracked down her mother, who

was dancing with her husband, Scott. Susan leaped at the sight of Amanda, her face contorting with pre-wedding anxiety.

"Are you heading out? Are you sure you can drive?"

Amanda hugged her mother, assuring her that she was sober, that she would see her soon, and that the wedding would be fine. It was funny. Most people felt they had to assure Amanda that everything was going to be all right, but Amanda knew she had to assure Susan instead. Amanda came by her hard-working attitude and her anxiety honestly.

Amanda hugged Audrey last, who blubbered that she wished they were heading back to the same place.

"I have to relieve the babysitter soon," Audrey said, yawning toward Noah, who sprung into action to find their things. "Where's Christine? We have the same sitter."

Deep in the party, Christine danced joyfully with her husband, Zach, with whom she'd had a baby named Mia. Unable to crawl through the entire crowd to get to her, Amanda waved, and Christine blew her a kiss. Beside her, Lola caught on and waved wildly, dancing with her sturdy sailor, Tommy Gasbarro.

Amanda got into the driver's side of Sam's car and buckled her seatbelt, watching the other guests turn on their vehicle lights and slowly depart the parking lot. Sam placed his hand on her thigh, and its warmth calmed her.

The cottage Sam and Amanda had purchased together in February had been a fixer-upper. Located about a mile down the coast from the Sheridan House, its exterior stones had been weathered from the harsh elements, and its windows had been cracked, some completely broken. An entire new porch had had to be installed.

It had felt like a big deal to buy a house with Sam. Amanda had hummed and hawed about it and even written a few pro and con lists, which was something she hadn't done in years. Ultimately, she'd done what Audrey had told her to do. "Follow your heart."

Amanda pulled the car into the driveway, turned off the engine, then kissed Sam in the dark shadows of the car. They stepped out, then headed up the walkway to the back porch, where they entered the house, removed their shoes, and immediately collapsed with exhaustion on the couch. The light of the moon shone through the window, where it hung above the Vineyard Sound. For a moment, Amanda listened to the late spring breeze as it rushed against the old house. Then, she hurried up to pour her and Sam glasses of water and pushed Sam the rest of the way to bed.

In their upstairs bedroom, Amanda and Sam brushed their teeth side-by-side and then snuggled into bed, where Sam fell asleep immediately. Amanda struggled, allowing herself a few moments of anxiety about the upcoming wedding, but then put herself to sleep again by telling herself every single detail she'd planned for the upcoming weekend.

Friday was the rehearsal dinner, which would take place at the Sunrise Cove to honor her Sheridan family roots. Her entire family and dear friends planned to attend the rehearsal dinner, including her father, Richard, who was bringing his new wife, Penelope. Penelope just happened to be the woman Richard had cheated on Susan with, but now that they'd had a child, Amanda had plowed her way through resentment and decided to welcome Penelope to her family.

Saturday would be a very long and life-altering day. There was no way to emotionally prepare for two hundred guests to watch you walk down the aisle and profess your love to a great man. Amanda planned to rely on adrenaline and champagne.

Chapter Five

The next morning at eight-thirty sharp, there was a tremendous banging at the door. Amanda groaned and rolled over, blinking through the morning light. "Sam? Do you hear that?"

Sam, who was probably very hungover after all that whiskey he'd drunk, rubbed his eyes and mumbled, "What?"

But the banging returned, this time more insistent than the last. Amanda hobbled out of bed and slumped toward the staircase, calling out, "I'm coming! Ugh."

Downstairs, Amanda opened the door to the porch that faced the driveway to find none other than Audrey Sheridan, bright-eyed and bushy-tailed, as though the last time Amanda had seen her (like seven hours ago), she hadn't been very drunk from too much rosé.

"Amanda!" Audrey lifted her arms and did a little jig. "Welcome to your surprise bachelorette party!"

Amanda leaned against the doorway, groaning and laughing at the same time. "You've got to be kidding me."

"I'm not!" Audrey snapped her fingers on both hands. "We've got a big show planned for you, our beautiful bride. Why don't you run off? Get showered? Pack up?"

"What do I need?" Amanda floundered.

Audrey answered vaguely. "You need everything for a perfect day on Martha's Vineyard, of course!"

By this time, Sam had stumbled the rest of the way down the staircase. He palmed the back of his neck and said, "Oh. Audrey. Hi."

Audrey placed her hands on her hips, pretending to be angry. "Sam, I thought I told you to have her ready by eight-thirty? It was literally the last thing I said to you last night!"

"You know better than to ask anything of Sam that late at night," Amanda said, grabbing Audrey's wrist to tug her into the house. "Give me ten minutes."

As Amanda scrambled around upstairs, she took the quickest shower she could, threw some things into a bag— her swimsuit, sun lotion, a big hat, sunglasses— then stepped out of her room to hear the noises downstairs of Sam brewing coffee and Audrey blabbing on about this and that.

"Max and Mia are both with Aunt Kerry, bless her. She seems to have a way with babies. I can't say I blamed Uncle Trevor when he made plans to be out of the house today, though. Ha."

Amanda dove down the steps to find Audrey and Sam at the breakfast table, where Sam had poured Amanda a cup of coffee. Amanda could have cried at the sight of two of her favorite people seated together as the morning light streamed beautifully through the window. Next week, this home would be her permanent place.

"You have to promise this will be a frequent scene," Amanda said to Audrey, her eyes widening as she sipped her coffee. "I want you to come over unannounced all the time."

"No problem," Audrey assured her. "But I already checked your cabinets. You're out of Pop Tarts."

Amanda kissed Sam goodbye, then headed out the door, hot on Audrey's heels. She then got into Audrey's car and braced herself for Audrey's rather wild driving, which whipped them away from the sea cottage, east toward Edgartown and then ever further east, toward the Katama Lodge and Wellness Spa.

"You're kidding," Amanda breathed.

"Come on. You and Aunt Susan have been insane with worry lately," Audrey said. "Mom and I thought it was only fitting if we start your bachelorette off with some relaxation. Saunas and massages for everyone!"

Susan, Aunt Christine, and Aunt Lola were already there, smiling happily as they drank coffee in the parking lot.

"Hi, honey." Susan hugged Amanda close. "I hope you're not too tired after last night?"

"Not at all," Amanda said. "It's wonderful to see all of you."

"Brittany and Brooke will be here later," Audrey said.

"For lunch," Lola affirmed. "They're meeting us at the Sheridan House."

Once inside, the Sheridan women changed into fluffy white robes and wandered into the warm coziness of the spa-side of the Katama Lodge, where women sat wrapped in towels in very hot rooms, their faces relaxed as tiny beads of sweat fell down their backs. Together, Amanda and Audrey stepped into a very hot sauna— 190 degrees Fahrenheit, and sat on the wood with their eyes closed. Two other women were in the room, which meant Amanda and Audrey had to remain very quiet, focusing on their breathing.

But when the two women abandoned the room and closed the door, Audrey burst. "Oh my gosh! It's too hot! I can't breathe!"

Amanda opened her eyes and laughed. "Yeah, it is. Every part of me is on slow mode."

"It's weird," Audrey said. "I've sweated out all the toxins from last night. Now, I'm working on all the toxins from last year."

Amanda giggled and leaned her head back, feeling her muscles loosen. Through the sauna's glass door, she watched Lola and Christine walk past in fluffy robes, carrying mugs of tea.

"This was such a good idea," Amanda said.

"There's more where this came from," Audrey assured her.

Amanda and Audrey stepped out into the crisp air, feeling a sense of relief wash over them. They strolled leisurely until they reached a picturesque blue pool where Susan, Christine, and Lola were gathered, enjoying themselves and savoring mouthwatering raspberries. Amanda settled down beside her mother, engrossed in the easy conversation flowing among the Sheridan sisters. They discussed Lola's aspirations to revamp the cozy cabin she shared with Tommy, Christine's recent decision to conclude breastfeeding Mia since she was now about a year and a half and no longer interested, and the exciting visit of Scott's son, Kellan, from university.

"Kellan's overjoyed to birdwatch with Dad again," Susan said. "He's taken a birdwatching seminar at the university level, but his knowledge still doesn't overshadow Dad's."

"I can't help but wonder how much Beatrice has changed him," Lola said. "He has so much more to live for now that he has someone to love. It feels like his dementia has stalled a bit."

"I think so, too," Christine said.

"It's probably been funny for the two of you to be roommates with your grandfather," Lola said, eyeing Audrey and Amanda.

Amanda and Audrey laughed knowingly, remembering hundreds of mornings they'd spent with their grandfather, teasing him just as much as he teased them. Yes, Amanda had had moments where she'd thought it was strange to live with this older man; where she'd looked at the dramatic tapestry of her life and wondered what had led her there. But she hadn't regretted it for a moment.

"It's been an unforgettable time of my life," Amanda said quietly. "I never even knew my grandfather during most of my life, and now he's one of my best friends."

"He's the weirdest and most wonderful man I've ever known," Audrey said.

"It's hard for me, sometimes, to acknowledge that I would never have really gotten to know him, or any of you, if I hadn't been left at the altar," Amanda went on. "Chris gave me a gift that day. It was just hard to recognize it at the time."

"I should have given him a knuckle sandwich," Lola said, half-joking. At least, Amanda thought she was half-joking. It was hard to know with Lola, who was a livewire.

After finishing at the Katama Lodge, they headed into the locker rooms to change back into their clothes and met in the glittering light outside the beautiful building. There, they said hello to Carmella and Elsa, whose father had opened the Katama Lodge many decades before. Elsa was engaged to Susan's colleague, Bruce, while Carmella had given birth last year and said she'd just returned to work.

"You must miss your daughter so much!" Christine said. "I hated going back to work after I had Mia."

Carmella placed her hand over her heart. "I count down the hours till I see Georgia again!"

The two mothers, both of whom hadn't had their first babies until their forties, locked eyes, understanding the weight of their later-in-life decisions and the tremendous happiness they'd built. Amanda swallowed a lump in her throat, overcome with empathy.

"All right! Next stop is the winery!" Lola clapped her hands and directed the women back to their vehicles, where she led the charge north of Edgartown to a place called The Hutton House, which was a boutique hotel and wine bar that stretched along the water. Like the Aquinnah Cliffside Hotel, it had been half-destroyed by a hurricane a couple of years back, but its owner, Olivia, had ensured it had been restored to its previous beauty. An islander herself, Olivia greeted the women happily and passed out wine lists. "My servers get annoyed with me when I talk to their tables," Olivia jested. "But one of the reasons I wanted to open this place was to chat with people like you!"

The Sheridan women opted for a bottle of natural

orange wine and a bottle of white, then ordered a charcuterie board with cured meats, camembert, cheddar, and gouda cheeses, plus dried and fresh fruits. Susan explained this was their snack before the "big lunch at home," which was being prepared for them.

"You are spoiling me!" Amanda cried.

"You deserve to be spoiled," Susan assured her. "Besides, when was the last time you had any fun? You've been working crazy hours at the law office and finishing up your law degree, all while taking care of the rest of us."

Amanda blushed. Truthfully, juggling so many things at once was the only way she knew to stay sane. Like Susan Sheridan before her, she needed every minute of her day to be packed with action, or else she got jittery and wondered what she was meant to do with her hands.

"Graduation was such a relief," Amanda said with a sigh, remembering just last month when her entire family had traveled to Rutgers to watch her walk across the graduation stage in her cap and gown. Although she'd done most of the coursework from Martha's Vineyard, she'd diligently completed her studies and graduated with a 4.0.

"What's next for you?" Christine asked.

"I guess we haven't made the official announcement yet," Susan said. "But Amanda is going to be a fully-fledged lawyer at the Sheridan Law Offices here in Martha's Vineyard, alongside Bruce and I."

"I've already handled a case on my own," Amanda admitted, her cheeks burning with a mix of pride and embarrassment.

"I still remember my first case by myself," Susan

breathed. "I was so green! So nervous! But I had good instincts, as you do, Amanda."

After a moment of silence, during which Susan beamed at her daughter with all the love in the world, Audrey waved her hand and said, "Enough of all this work talk. This is a bachelorette party, isn't it? Are you ready for the first game?"

"What game?" Amanda asked.

"I invented it," Audrey said.

"Oh no." Amanda groaned into laughter, always nervous yet excited when Audrey got creative with something.

"We're in public, Audrey," Susan reminded her. "Nothing too... adult."

Audrey rolled her eyes, then said, "Fine. We can play that later. For now, we can focus on the Newlywed Game." She removed her phone from her pocket, then waved it. "I asked Sam a series of questions. If Amanda can answer how he answered correctly, we have to drink. If she can't answer, she has to drink."

"Except for me," Susan said. "I'm the driver."

"Typical Susan. Always there for us," Lola teased, then hugged her sister from the side.

"All right. Ready for the first question?" Audrey asked.

"As I'll ever be," Amanda said.

"What is Sam's favorite book?"

Amanda laughed. "Easy. *Farewell to Arms* by Ernest Hemingway."

"Very good."

"Literary fiancé," Christine teased.

Amanda beamed, remembering the long nights she

and Sam had spent side-by-side, their thighs touching as they dove through books, both together and separately.

"Next question," Audrey said. "This one's a toughie."

"Shoot."

"I asked Sam what his last meal would be if he could choose," Audrey said. "What did he say?"

"Steak? I think. With macaroni and cheese."

"And..." Audrey's eyes widened.

"Something else?" Amanda asked.

"He added a dessert," Audrey hinted.

"Wow. Um. Tiramisu?"

"Ding, ding, ding! Ladies, Amanda knows Sam through and through. We're going to be very tipsy by the end of this game," Audrey said.

When they returned to the Sheridan House later that afternoon, Amanda's two best friends from Newark were out on the back porch, along with Claire, Charlotte, Rachel, Gail, Abby, and Lexi. Amanda dove through the porch, hugging everyone and thanking them for throwing her such a beautiful party. When she reached her best friends from Newark, she shrieked with joy at seeing them, demanding that they spend some time catching up. "I barely know anything that's going on in your lives," Amanda said, wincing at all the time they'd allowed to pass between calls.

Inside the house, Christine's husband, Zach, finished up their delectable lunch of goat cheese salads, salmon, potatoes cooked with rosemary, and lemon cake. As he finished plating the last of the salmon, he waved at Amanda and said, "I think this is the first bachelorette party I've ever been invited to."

Christine hurried over to Zach to kiss him, then said, "And it's just about time you left, don't you think?"

Zach laughed and wrapped his arms around Christine. "She loves me so much. Isn't it clear?" he asked Amanda.

"I think Mia needs you," Amanda said.

"Super dad, at your service," Zach said. "I'll see you later. Don't do anything I wouldn't do."

Amanda and her friends and family gathered on the back porch, indulging in a delightful spread of nourishing and vibrant dishes. They savored the flavors, replenished their glasses with wine, and enjoyed the tranquil spectacle of three sailboats gracefully dancing on the horizon, seemingly engaged in a playful pursuit under the radiant sun. The atmosphere was filled with warmth and contentment as they shared this picturesque moment together.

"Kelli just texted to ask how we're doing," Charlotte said across the table, her rosé lifted. "She wishes she could be here for you, Amanda."

"I'm sure she's so stressed," Amanda said, remembering how panicked Kelli had looked last night at the hotel.

"I wonder if she bit off more than she can chew?" Claire suggested, grimacing.

"I think she wants to prove to herself that she can do this," Charlotte said. "Especially after everything that happened with Mike."

"A divorce definitely makes you second-guess yourself," Susan agreed. "I wanted to come here and start my own law office and 'prove' to myself that I didn't need Richard in the first place."

"And you did that," Christine pointed out.

"Yes, but there were times when I nearly fell over with exhaustion," Susan said. "I'm so glad that difficult time of my life is over. I'm sure Kelli will look back at this time in the same way." Susan sipped her wine, then added, "But the hotel is absolutely stunning, isn't it? Scott told me that Kelli picked out almost all the furniture and the art. I think it's the perfect location for Amanda's wedding."

"Everything is going to be perfect," Lola agreed, her eyes dancing.

"Better than perfect," Charlotte said. "I'm the wedding planner, after all. It's up to me to make it so."

Chapter Six

It was Monday morning. Kelli stood at the hotel's front desk with her head bowed as she skimmed through the photographs Charlotte had posted on social media from the bachelorette party over the weekend. In them, her beautiful family members ate, drank, and laughed in front of the water, occasionally in swimsuits, their eyes getting increasingly glossy as the day wore on. In one that seemed to have been taken much later in the day, Amanda wore a floral headband and held a bottle of champagne, one arm slung around Audrey. They laughed as though it was the only thing they knew how to do.

Kelli's stomach felt very cold. She'd missed a genuinely beautiful weekend with family because she'd been needed here.

Since Saturday's opening, Kelli had spent little more than a few hours at a time away from the hotel. Last night, she'd managed to leave around one in the morning, but had awoken three hours later, slick with sweat, worrying about an order that was supposed to arrive that morning.

Had she remembered to tell Piper to be there early to receive it? She couldn't remember. So, she'd jumped in the shower, done her makeup, and returned to find Piper there, bright and early, saying, "I thought you told me to be here for the package!"

But Kelli had been up and ready, so she'd thrown herself into the numerous other tasks that seemed never-ending. She'd begun to wonder if she would ever have a normal, non-panicked thought again.

One thing she hadn't fully anticipated was how little guests seemed to respect the staff. More than once, she witnessed guests berating staff members for "not carrying their suitcases correctly" or "not being prompt with the valet of their vehicles." This bothered Kelli a great deal. Yes, the guests were of the richer variety of Martha's Vineyard vacationers, but where was their empathy?

"How are you doing?" Susan asked Piper privately after lunch, right after a woman had come down from room seventy-seven to complain about the draft in the hallway.

"I'm fine," Piper said, her eyes a little too large.

"That woman wasn't very nice," Kelli pointed out.

"That's just hospitality," Piper said. "I've worked at hotels for years, as you know. I've found ways to let those complaints roll off of me."

"Do you have any tips?" Kelli asked.

Piper laughed. "Just give yourself some time. You'll find your own way through this."

Kelli wasn't so sure.

Around three, Xander arrived at the hotel to help Kelli with some important paperwork. Together, they sat in the safety of her office and held each other as Kelli mumbled all her worries. Xander said all the right things, then hurried downstairs to ask the chef to make Kelli a sandwich and a salad.

"You need to take care of yourself," he told her as he placed the food on her desk. "I'm going to sit right here until you finish all of it."

Kelli rolled her eyes. "Are you my mother?"

"I'm not. But if you want me to call Kerry Montgomery right now and ask her what she thinks about you eating that sandwich, I will."

"You'd really use Kerry Montgomery against me?" Kelli asked with a laugh.

"Don't try me."

Unfortunately for Kelli's sanity, Xander had to head out around seven to meet a business associate who was on the Vineyard for just that night. Kelli again found herself in the madness of an evening at a brand-new luxury hotel, her feet aching and the inside of her mind a scream.

This all came to a head around nine-thirty when a man appeared at the front desk. He wore a name-brand suit jacket and Italian leather shoes, and he stared at his fingernails as he spoke to Piper.

"My mother is really quite upset with her room," he said in an English accent.

Kelli, who stood behind Piper, perked up her ears, sensing that there was something really off about this guy.

"I'm sorry to hear that. Can you be more specific?" Piper said.

The man sounded bored. "Something or other with her room, or her bathroom, or a window. I'm not quite sure. Could you send someone up to check?"

"Certainly, sir. And is there anything we can do for you this evening?" Piper asked.

"I'll be at the bar," the man said. "My mother is in room 401."

Piper, ever professional, sent two employees up to the man's mother's suite, where they found nothing really wrong. But within the hour, the man returned to the desk again to say that his mother continued to complain of something in her room.

"She's threatening to check out of it isn't worked out," the man said, sounding bored.

Kelli was flabbergasted. She stepped beside Piper and said, "We sent our employees up to your mother's room to check on your mother, but she seemed fine. Is she telling you something that she isn't telling us?"

The man shrugged simply and said, "I'm sure you wouldn't want my mother to tell her very affluent friends how flippant this hotel has been with her needs." He then returned to the bar, where he ordered a double scotch and gave his full attention to his phone.

Kelli took a deep breath, reminding herself that this hotel was her dream, then decided to go up to room 401 by herself to ensure the older woman was taken care of. She took the stairs, using the time to focus on her breathing, then knocked on the door to find a woman in her mid-seventies, her hair a shining silver and her robe a similar shade, clearly expensive, as though it had recently been spun by silkworms.

"Good evening," Kelli said with a smile. "I hope it's not too late to disturb you. Your son has informed us that you've had a difficult night, and I wanted to make sure that you're all right. Is there anything we can do?"

The woman had beady eyes that seemed to go straight through Kelli, whom she probably didn't deem "rich enough." "Yes. I've struggled endlessly to get this television to play what I need it to play."

Kelli swallowed, trying not to spin-out with rage. She was the manager of this hotel— it wasn't up to her to fix people's televisions, was it? With a smile, she stepped into the woman's ornate suite, which Kelli herself had decorated with gorgeous artwork and sublime curtains, then picked up the remote control to adjust the television to play what the woman wanted.

"Isn't that nice," the woman said, although she didn't sound pleased.

"Is that all you need?" Kelli asked.

"I suppose so." The woman placed bifocals on her nose and sat at the edge of her bed, no longer interested in Kelli's presence.

Flabbergasted, Kelli bid the woman goodnight, then headed into the hallway. But just after she'd clipped the door closed, it opened again, and that same woman peered out at her.

"Miss?" The woman blinked.

"Do you need something else?" Kelli wanted to fall to the floor and weep.

"It's just that I expected turn-down service," the woman said. "And I haven't received that yet."

Unfortunately, Kelli was suddenly reminded of all the items on her to-do list, of all the horrifically time-consuming things she had to do when she reached her office. When would she ever have time to sleep?

Just before she lost her nerve, however, Sandra swooped in from the left, all bright and smiley, and said, "I'm happy to do your turn-down service, Miss Jennings."

Kelli breathed deeply, locking eyes with the twenty-something staff member she'd just met the other day, the one who'd saved her after her shoe had broken.

"Sandra," Kelli said, as Miss Jennings receded into her hotel room. "You're a lifesaver!"

Sandra waved her hand. "It's no trouble. I heard a rumor that you've been at the hotel for fifty-plus hours since Saturday. Why don't you go home? Get some shut-eye?"

Kelli blinked at the young woman, incredulous. "No wonder you're friends with Amanda," she said finally. "She's always looking out for people, just like you."

"It's my job," Sandra corrected. "But yes. I hope I have a tiny bit of Amanda Harris' kindness and compassion." She then waved as she passed through Miss Jennings' doorway, prepared to give her the service she needed to get to bed.

And although Kelli remained at the hotel another thirty minutes after that, neither Miss Jennings nor her son complained again.

That night, Kelli collapsed in bed just a few minutes before Xander returned home. After he removed his clothes, he clambered into bed after her and curled himself around her, cuddling her.

"How was the rest of your day, baby?"

Kelli tried her best not to cry. "This is so much harder than I thought it would be. And the guests all have minds of their own!"

"Hospitality is a beast," Xander said. "But remember what we talked about? About you hiring someone to pick up your slack? It's purely selfish, of course. I just want you here more often."

"I'm sure you want me sane, too," Kelli said.

"I don't need you to be sane, but I think it's more comfortable for both of us."

Kelli giggled, in her first good mood of the day, then kissed Xander gently with her eyes closed.

After a long, comfortable pause, Kelli settled her head back on the pillow and said, "I've been really impressed with this newcomer to the island. Amanda's friend, who happens to work up at the hotel."

"What's her name?"

"Sandra," Kelli remembered. "Maybe I could finagle a way for her and Piper to be my second-in-command staff."

"Wow. Look at you, learning to delegate."

Kelli elbowed his stomach, making him laugh. "I'm serious, Kelli! Delegation is supposedly the number-one thing good leaders learn how to do. If I was a leader, I would delegate all the time. But as you know, I work for myself and don't really play well with others. Except you, of course."

"And I appreciate your help every single day," Kelli said as she slowly drifted off to sleep, already breathing easier. Very soon, she would structure the Aquinnah Cliffside Overlook Hotel staff workload to allow herself more time with Xander, more time to sit comfortably in the ballroom at the hotel and dream about the hotel's dramatic past, and more time to just feel the peace that had come this late in her forties. It was time.

Chapter Seven

Tuesday morning, Amanda awoke at the Sheridan House at six-thirty, tied her hair into a ponytail, grabbed her yoga mat, and hurried out the door. The drive to the yoga studio in downtown Oak Bluffs took seven minutes, which got her there at six-fifty-five, just in time to get a good spot up front. Just like always as of late, Sandra was there just a split-second before Amanda, already sitting cross-legged on her yoga mat.

"Hi!" Sandra patted the space beside her. "Everyone knows that I reserve the space beside me for you now. They don't even try to sit by me."

Amanda laughed as she set up her yoga mat.

"How are you feeling?" Sandra asked. "Just a few more days till the wedding!"

"I know. I'm so nervous," Amanda confessed.

"Why? It's going to go so well!"

Amanda eyed the door as a few more yogies straggled in, all looking as though they'd just hobbled from bed.

"My ex-fiancé left me at the altar," Amanda confessed to Sandra very quietly.

All the blood drained from Sandra's cheeks. "You're kidding! That's horrible, Amanda. I'm so sorry."

Amanda shrugged. "It was probably for the best. I mean, if he hadn't left, I never would have met Sam. And Sam's my everything."

Sandra nodded, although her eyes still glinted with pity, which Amanda hated. "Where is your ex-fiancé now?"

"He was traveling a lot," Amanda remembered. "He went to Thailand, Argentina, India, and eight thousand places in between."

"Were you jealous?" Sandra asked.

"No," Amanda admitted. "I never wanted to travel. I always wanted to settle down, have a family, and focus on my career, the way my mother did. Isn't that boring?"

"I don't think so." Sandra frowned.

Amanda eyed the door, wondering where the yoga instructor was. She was a minute late, which wasn't like her. "What about you, Sandra?" Amanda asked. "I've been babbling about my wedding to Sam since we met, but I hardly know anything about you. Are you seeing anyone?"

Sandra's face was suddenly dreamy. "I'm very in love, actually."

"Wow! I had no idea. Who is he?"

"My fiancé is a really wonderful man. I met him several years ago, but we were separated for a while, which was devastating. When he got back, it was like we immediately picked back up again and got engaged shortly after," Sandra explained.

"That's beautiful. Is he here on the island?" Amanda asked.

"He will be soon," Sandra explained. "We're planning our future and can't wait to settle down and have kids, just like you."

"That's incredible," Amanda said, her heart opening at the happiness in her new friend's eyes. "What does he do?"

"Oh, he's in art dealing," Sandra explained. "He has a tremendous eye for detail. Sometimes, at art museums, he'll talk to me about what makes a painting or a drawing or a piece of jewelry special for half an hour. He usually knows more than the people who work there."

"I wouldn't know the first thing about that," Amanda said. "He sounds really special."

"Sorry, I'm late!" The yoga instructor burst into the room, her cheeks a violent red. "I hate to admit this, but I overslept. Now. Everyone, take some deep breaths while I set up!"

Amanda and Sandra exchanged knowing smiles, both aware that they weren't the type to ever sleep past their alarms. Still, they would forgive the yoga instructor for this faux pas. It didn't really matter, anyway.

Back at home, Amanda showered, did her hair, and brewed a pot of coffee, listening as the house awoke around her. It was eight-thirty, and Grandpa Wes appeared in the kitchen, his smile big and happy as he said, "Just four more days till the wedding, Amanda!"

Amanda poured her grandfather a mug of coffee. "Do you think you'll be able to come?" she asked him, teasing.

"I hope I can squeeze it in," Grandpa Wes said. "I have a busy schedule, you know."

"Don't I know it."

Audrey appeared after that, Max on her hip. Now almost two and a half, Max was eager to speak and frequently babbled, making up little stories that nobody really understood.

"We went to the car college," he told Amanda simply as Audrey put him in his highchair.

"The car college, huh?" Amanda sliced strawberries, kiwis, and bananas for the four of them, filling a bowl.

"Yes. Max loves talking about the car college. If only I knew what that was!" Audrey laughed.

"That's where we see the cars," Max said simply.

Audrey hunted through a toy box in the corner to find one of Max's favorite toys, a green car that he now rolled along his highchair table as he made "pew, pew, pew" sounds.

"How was yoga?" Audrey asked.

"It was great. You should really come with me sometime," Amanda said.

"Yes. If I ever have a lobotomy and lose my sense of self completely, I will come to yoga with you," Audrey said.

Grandpa Wes sat at the breakfast table with his newspaper and a big bowl of fruit and yogurt, reading the news as, beside him, his phone exploded with text messages. Although Amanda told herself not to look, she did spot Beatrice's name before she fully forced her eyes away.

"Someone really wants to reach out to you today," Audrey teased as she fed Max, who was already covered in yogurt.

"What? Oh." Grandpa Wes lit up as he raised his phone to read the texts. He then laughed to himself, as though Beatrice had told him the most delicious joke.

"You're so cheesy, Grandpa," Audrey said.

"We're all cheesy," Amanda reminded her. "We're all hopelessly in love and pathetic about it. Right, Max?"

Max smacked his palm through a mound of yogurt so that it exploded across his bib. Audrey smiled and reached for a paper towel, never one to linger on the messiness of her son. She was the perfect toddler mother in that she hardly minded messes and was very quick to wave her sorrows away.

As Audrey cleaned up Max's face, she turned to lock eyes with Amanda for a moment, and Amanda's heart thudded with sudden sorrow. This was one of the final breakfasts with her favorite breakfast crew. This was the final week of her single life.

It struck her that time would continue to pass, that their grandfather would get older, and that his dementia would eventually rear its ugly head. Max would even, one day, probably run off to college and take on the world. Where would Amanda be at that point? Would she and Audrey always be this close? Or would time have its way with them, the way it did with everything and everyone else?

Amanda decided to walk to the Sheridan Law Office that morning. She packed her heels in her backpack and strode in tennis shoes, her sunglasses protecting her from the bright June light. As she entered downtown Oak Bluffs, islanders waved to her, congratulating her on her upcoming wedding.

Once at the law office, Amanda greeted their intern, Mallory, and entered her office, where she watered the plants and then got to work on her brand-new case, which involved a man who'd been accused of manslaughter. It was not an easy case to stomach, but Amanda knew that to be a defense attorney, she had to be strong. She couldn't let the evils of the world get to her. The law was the law, a collection of rules and public obligations, one that gave her a sense of safety. It boggled her mind, sometimes, that people didn't look at the law in the same way.

At lunch, Amanda sat outside the harbor with a sandwich, when Claire called with questions about the finalization of Amanda's bouquet for Saturday.

"Hi, honey! I'm sorry to bother you so close to Saturday," Claire said.

"Not a problem. What's up?"

"I have a note here regarding the flowers you want on both your bouquet and the bridesmaid bouquets. But before I make anything, I have to tell you that I just got a specialty order of peonies in."

Amanda leaned forward so quickly that she nearly dropped her sandwich. Every bride knew how beautiful it was to have peonies on her wedding day— and every bride on a budget knew how ridiculous it was to ask for that. Obviously, Amanda's budget was much easier than others', given that Kelli had offered up the hotel for free, Charlotte was planning the wedding for free, and Claire was doing the bouquets for free. But because Claire had been so kind about that, Amanda had chosen budget florals to ensure she didn't break Claire's bank.

"Are you sure?" Amanda coughed.

"Honey, of course! It's your wedding day. And you know how much our family loves Sam." Claire paused for a moment, then added, "I was thinking I could focus on peonies for your bouquet and then add just a few for the bachelorettes'."

"That is beyond my wildest dreams," Amanda said.

"And some flowers for your mother, of course," Claire

said. "Someone mentioned Susan is walking you down the aisle?"

"I asked her," Amanda said, "but she said she wants to think about it. I don't think she wants to push my father out of the limelight if you can believe it."

"Oh gosh. Well, what do you think about that?" Claire wasn't sure what to say, although Amanda knew that every Sheridan had very little respect for Richard Harris.

"I think I'd better clear this up with my mother," Amanda said.

"Do," Claire urged her. "I need to know exactly what kind of floral arrangement your mother needs, given her role in the ceremony. It's four days away, Amanda!"

Amanda assured Claire she'd clear everything up soon, then got off the phone, finished her sandwich, and retreated back to her office for another few hours of work. En route, she paused outside Susan's office and waved.

Susan raised her finger as she finished a conversation with someone over the phone. "I have no interest in representing Franklin Butler. I've told you that numerous times."

Amanda raised her eyebrows, impressed. Franklin Butler was the once-famed billionaire of Martha's Vineyard, who was now infamous due to his manipulation of women like Mandy Dolores, who'd gone missing that spring. Luckily, Mr. Butler's outrageous acts hadn't resulted in any casualties. Still, he had stabbed Isabella's boyfriend along the way.

When Susan got off the phone, she shook her head. "I don't see why that man won't catch a hint. All I've done, over and over, is tell his people that I don't care to represent him."

"He knows you would get him a decreased sentence," Amanda said, leaning through the doorway.

"I have no interest in helping him." Susan's face was marred with worry before she lifted her eyes and righted her smile. "Can I help you with something, honey?"

Amanda said she wanted to have dinner with her mother that evening if Susan had the time. Susan all-but sang with excitement.

"I can't believe the bride has time for me this week! Somebody, pinch me."

At five-thirty sharp, Susan and Amanda walked to a little wine bar in downtown Oak Bluffs with a view of the water and sat together over the menu, trying to figure out which white wine suited them that evening. As Susan studied the menu, her eyes focused, Amanda swam with nostalgia. It felt as though everything in this week glittered with emotion, as though she was seeing it with these eyes for the last time.

Susan and Amanda ordered a bottle of Pinot Grigio, pecorino cheese, and green olives, telling the waiter they'll order dinner later. As they settled into their seats overlooking the water, Amanda finally got up the nerve to ask her mother the question on her mind.

"Mom? Remember how you said you weren't sure you should walk me down the aisle? That you didn't want to step on Dad's toes?"

Susan turned her head slightly. "I remember."

"Well, the thing is, I never asked Dad," Amanda continued, feeling strangely nervous, as though she'd done something wrong. "And I'm still pretty set on you walking me down."

Susan closed her eyes for a moment, as though she

was overwhelmed. Amanda laced her fingers through her mother's, waiting.

"I mean, only if you really don't mind," Amanda said again.

When Susan opened her eyes again, they glinted with tears. "Oh, honey. It would be my greatest privilege. I just didn't want you to regret anything."

"Why would I regret you walking me down the aisle?" Amanda asked.

"I always thought you were rooted in traditional ways. Always thought you wanted to do everything by the book," Susan tried. "You used to cry when our routines weren't exactly right when you were a kid."

"Nothing about my life the past few years has been by the book," Amanda pointed out. "And I've preferred it that way."

Susan's smile widened.

"Trust me. I'm just as surprised as you are about that," Amanda said.

"If you really don't mind, I'd love to walk you down the aisle," Susan breathed. "It will be the greatest privilege of my life."

Chapter Eight

Wednesday morning at the Aquinnah Cliffside Overlook Hotel, Kelli did a final look-through of Sandra's resume to see that she had sufficient training in hotel management and past experience to allow Kelli to make her a sort of middle-manager. She then called both Piper and Sandra into her office to happily announce that she wanted to give them both promotions.

Across the desk, Piper and Sandra sat with beautiful, twenty-something smiles, both eager to move up the ranks at this brand-new, exclusive hotel.

"Are you serious?" Sandra leaned forward in her chair, genuinely shocked.

"I accept," Piper said firmly.

"You both need to get better at this side of business. What should you have asked me first?" Kelli asked.

Piper and Sandra eyed one another, confused.

"The money!" Kelli said. "You should have asked me what the raise was going to be."

"Oh!" Sandra laughed. "Gosh. I don't know. It feels a little forward, doesn't it?"

"As women, we shouldn't be afraid to ask for what we're worth," Kelli said, paraphrasing an article she'd just read about "women in business" from *The Atlantic*. "I've just told both of you that I want to move you up the ranks." Kelli waited for one of them to say a number, anything to indicate what they required monetarily for this new role, but neither of them knew what to say.

Kelli understood this very well. She'd spent most of her life thinking she wasn't worth anything: not a very good salary, nor a kind, romantic partner. Xander had helped with both.

Eventually, Kelli told both Piper and Sandra what she'd been considering for their pay raises, and both of them leaped at it, genuinely over the moon. Afterward, Kelli outlined the responsibilities she felt each would excel at, dividing them up to allow herself more hours of shut-eye, more time with her kids, and more of a romantic and free life with Xander. She was in charge of the hotel, of course, but she didn't want to go full Jack Nicholson in *The Shining*.

Before Kelli finished, she reached into her pocket to find the second master key, which she handed off to Piper. "I'll give this to you, Piper. Sandra, if you don't mind, I'll have a new one made for you by next week."

"Of course not," Sandra said with a smile as Piper pocketed the key.

"We'll get better at asking for raises later on," Piper joked as they stood to return to their responsibilities. "Especially as our confidence here at the hotel grows." She winked, and Kelli laughed, genuinely grateful for Piper's peppy mood and great sense of humor.

A Vineyard Love

"Thank you so much," Sandra said, lingering by the door for a moment. "I never could have imagined how much Martha's Vineyard would change my life."

Kelli smiled to herself for the rest of the morning, relaxing into her life at the hotel now that she'd handed out her responsibilities. When Xander called her around noon to ask if she had plans for dinner, she said, "I don't!"

Xander suggested that he meet her at the hotel around seven-thirty for dinner. Kelli was pleased. It had been a while since she'd been able to sit in that immaculate ballroom and genuinely appreciate the glorious old place. For nearly two years, she'd romanticized her grandmother's love for her grandfather, there in the walls of that old hotel, and now, she wanted to pretend to live that love.

Before dinner, Kelli dressed into a beautiful black dress that was cut slightly lower over her chest than most she braved to wear, then did her makeup carefully. She knew that tonight, all eyes of staff and guests would be upon her and Xander, as they knew that Xander and Kelli owned and operated the hotel together. They were a power couple. They were having dinner there to support the hotel, in a way, as though they were movie stars who needed to promote their recent film.

Kelli had never done anything to be seen before. It wasn't really in her nature. But with Xander's gorgeous suits and Kelli's newfound success in the hotelier world, she saw no reason not to try it. Maybe it would be fun. Maybe it would be like acting.

Xander met Kelli in the foyer of the hotel and wrapped his arms around her lower back. There, in the echoing foyer lined with mahogany wood and stylish paintings, Xander kissed Kelli with his eyes closed. Kelli couldn't tell if this was an act or genuine— if he wanted to prove his love to her in front of so many, or if he just genuinely felt that love in his soul.

"That was something," Kelli said as the kiss broke.

Xander laughed. "Should I wait for those kinds of kisses till we get home?"

"Not necessarily."

Kelli and Xander walked toward the dining room, where the host greeted them and led them to the owners' table. Naturally, the owners' table had the best view of both the ballroom and the cliffs outside and had been set with the finest china and the whitest tablecloth. When Kelli and Xander didn't plan on eating at the restaurant, the dining table was always empty, just in case they popped in for a surprise dinner. "That," Xander had said once, "is what you want from owning a hotel. Isn't it?"

The host lit the candle between Kelli and Xander and took their wine order— the very best red they had in the cellar.

"We're celebrating," Xander said mischievously as the host hurried away.

"What are we celebrating?"

"We're celebrating your first free time of the week," Xander said, as though that was obvious. "I couldn't help but see the fresh fish they brought in this morning— salmon and sea bass and octopus. It looked delicious. I think we should order as many dishes as we can until we're stuffed. What do you think?"

Kelli could do nothing but follow the night. Tiny plates featuring the delectable dishes cooked up by Chef Billiard and his team came to their table, one after another, in a stream of flavor and inventive pairings. Throughout, Xander and Kelli talked easily, swapped jokes, and glowed with impossible joy.

Just after the salmon dish arrived at the table, and Kelli's head swam with delectable wine, two police officers appeared in the doorway to the restaurant. Immediately, Kelli sobered up, straightening her spine as she rose.

"What's up?" Xander turned to follow her gaze as Kelli's heart pounded.

Terribly, her first thought was of Mike, her ex-husband. *How could he have possibly hurt her again? How could she have allowed that?* But Mike was miles away from the hotel, away from the island, in prison for stealing funds from the town of Oak Bluffs. He couldn't hurt her all the way out here. *Could he?*

"I'm going to talk to them," Kelli said. "Eat the salmon."

"Not without you," Xander assured her and leaped to his feet, following her across the ballroom to greet the officers.

"Evening, Kelli." Bobby, the first officer, stepped back to lead Kelli deeper into the foyer.

"Evening," Kelli said. "Bobby. Tristan. What's this about?"

"Why don't we step into your office?" Bobby suggested. "It's a delicate matter."

Kelli's heart pounded. Xander paused for a moment to tell the host that they needed to leave their table and to return the salmon to the kitchen for the time being. Afterward, Kelli and Xander led the officers to the back staircase, which they took to Kelli's office.

"I hope everything's okay?" Kelli sounded timid as she rounded her desk and sat. Xander remained standing beside her.

Bobby and Tristan shifted uneasily in front of them.

"We got an anonymous tip regarding one of your employees," Bobby began. "Piper Billings?"

Kelli frowned. "Piper's a fantastic employee. I just promoted her to middle-manager."

"It seems that she's been involved in criminal dealings here on the island," Bobby went on.

"What kind of criminal dealings?" Kelli demanded.

"We aren't at liberty to reveal that at this time," Bobby said. "Suffice it to say, we wouldn't recommend that she remain here at the hotel. She seems dangerous."

Kelli's eyes widened. All she could think of was beautiful Piper, who treated all the guests with patience and kindness and genuinely kept Kelli above water when she struggled.

"That's impossible," Kelli suggested.

"It's true, ma'am," Tristan chimed in. "Piper Billings could possibly turn out to be the mastermind of a string of robberies across the island. I wouldn't be surprised if she's currently figuring out new and creative ways to take from this very hotel."

Kelli's heartbeat quickened. *How was this possible? Hadn't she looked at every background check herself? Hadn't she and Piper just swapped recipes that morning, laughing as the sunlight glittered through the two-story windows around the ballroom?*

"Do you have proof?" Kelli asked.

Bobby nodded. "We're gathering evidence against her and plan to make an arrest within the next few days."

"But we wanted to give you a heads-up first," Tristan explained. "This hotel's success is important to the island. We don't want some wayward criminal making a mess of things."

Kelli couldn't breathe. "I just promoted her. I just gave her the master key!"

"I would take that away from her as quickly as you can," Tristan urged her.

"We can stay right here until then," Bobby said.

"I don't know. I don't want her to feel like I'm accusing her of anything yet," Kelli said. "If she walks into my office and two cops are behind my desk, she'll..." Kelli trailed off, embarrassed of what she wanted to say. In truth, she just didn't want Piper to hate her. A part of her heart still considered Piper a friend.

"We could step into the closet," Bobby said, glancing at the door to the right of Kelli's desk. "Just in case things go south."

Kelli nodded, feeling at a loss. Just hours ago, she'd figured out how to delegate— and she'd managed to delegate to a wanted criminal. *How could she have gotten it so wrong?*

After the officers were safely concealed in her closet, Kelli texted Piper to say she needed to see her in her office. Xander wanted to stay, but Kelli shooed him out, saying that it would look strange with both of them there. "Go! Eat the salmon. Someone has to."

"I'll wait for you," Xander said before he disappeared.

When Piper breezed through the door, her ponytail bounced, and she chatted excitedly about Miss Jennings, the old woman from Room 401 who hadn't been able to stop complaining since her arrival the previous weekend.

"I just don't know why she wants to stay here a day more. You would have thought she was in prison or something," Piper said.

Kelli took a deep breath. *How could Piper act so flippantly? Was this her way of manipulating her?*

"Piper, I'm sorry to do this, but I have to let you go." Kelli pressed her lips together but continued to stare Piper in the eye. She wanted to be respectful in some way, even as she fired this young woman.

Immediately, Piper's face crumpled. She let out a small laugh, then asked, "Are you joking?"

Kelli bristled. She watched the young woman go through many stages of fear, then acceptance before she collapsed in the chair across from the desk. "Did I do something wrong?" Piper's voice was so frail, without any of the peppiness she normally offered the hotel guests.

"Do you have your master key? I would like that immediately." Kelli placed both of her hands on her desk and blinked at Piper, trying not to evoke any emotion, even as her heart shattered in her chest.

Piper's hand shook as she removed her key from her pocket and placed it on the desk. She looked completely at a loss.

"Please, Kelli. As a friend. Just tell me what I did, so that I won't do it again at the next place. It's the least you can do."

But Kelli had very little information from the officers. More than that, it was difficult for her to imagine Piper stealing anything, not even a packet of chewing gum. Maybe this was the genius of Piper. Maybe she understood she could get away with anything because she was friendly and beautiful and young.

"Please, go to the break room, get your things, and leave as quickly as possible," Kelli said. "Your payment should be transferred to your account by the end of the month. I wish you luck in your future endeavors."

Piper gaped at her for a long moment, then stood in a huff and walked out the door, looking like a wounded animal. After the door was closed safely behind her, Kelli placed her face in her hands and allowed herself to cry. She'd forgotten that the officers were watching her on the other side of the door. When they revealed themselves, she tidied herself up and shook their hands, saying, "Thank you for your diligent work. This is my first week as a hotel manager, and I can already tell I'm making about a thousand mistakes per day."

"It'll get easier," Bobby assured her. "Especially now that you have that criminal out of your midst."

After Bobby and Tristan walked downstairs, already muttering about their plans to arrest Piper officially over the next few days, Kelli rubbed her temples and eventually got up the nerve to text Sandra, the only other person in the hotel who needed to know about Piper.

Sandra arrived a few minutes later, bright and cheery, her cheeks like apples. "I was just in Miss Jennings' room," she explained as she sat across from Kelli and crossed her ankles. "That woman just doesn't know how to have a good time, does she? I want to ask her, 'Have you seen how beautiful this room is? Have you even bothered to look at it?'" Sandra chuckled adorably.

Kelli struggled to match Sandra's enthusiasm. It occurred to her, now, that she'd never fired anyone before, and it had felt a bit like punching herself in the face.

"What's wrong, Kelli?" Sandra's face transformed. "You look a bit sick."

"I wanted to let you know first-thing that I've had to let Piper go," Kelli explained.

Sandra's face now matched Kelli's stricken feeling. "Are you serious? What happened!"

"The police came to let me know they suspect she's been involved in criminal activity across the island. They're preparing to arrest her over the next few days," she said.

"Piper?" Sandra's eyes widened with shock. "That doesn't make any sense."

Kelli raised her shoulders. "All we can do is press forward as we have been, but without the help of Piper."

"But you just gave Piper that middle-manager position," Sandra said softly. "You were just having dinner downstairs with Xander!"

Kelli now felt that the dinner with Xander had been a part of a dream, and she'd awoken to return to the frantic nightmare of her life. "I'll hire someone to fill Piper's position soon. In the meantime, it'll just be you and I keeping this hotel afloat. Remember that this weekend is my cousin's daughter's wedding, which will be a doozy. She has over two hundred guests coming, most of whom are staying at the hotel itself. Decorations, cake, food, and so much more will be arriving on a crazy-looking schedule that my sister, the wedding planner, just sent me via email. Maybe I can forward the email to you?"

Sandra set her jaw, her eyes stormy and serious. "Send it my way. I'll be here as much as you need me, Kelli. I promise you that we will get through this. Together."

Kelli blinked back tears, telling herself to believe in Sandra's fortitude. She then reached for Piper's master key and passed it across the desk to Sandra, who held it, glinting, in her right hand.

"You'll need this," Kelli told her. "Like I told Piper earlier today, it opens every single door in the entire hotel.

Do not lose it. It's important that it doesn't fall into the wrong hands."

"I'll trust it with my life," Sandra assured her. "Thank you for this opportunity, Kelli. I won't let you down."

Chapter Nine

Friday morning, Amanda found herself at the Oak Bluffs harbor in a little white sundress, her eyes to the horizon. The boat that surged toward her carried Richard, Penelope, Jake, Kristen, and Jake and Kristen's three kids. According to a text from her father, Penelope and Richard had left their child with Penelope's mother to ensure an easier passage that weekend. "I want this weekend to be all about you, Amanda," her father had written, which had been nice, she supposed. He got points for that.

Amanda was apprehensive, as she still hadn't told her father that she wanted Susan to walk her down the aisle instead of him. More than that, though, she was nervous to see her father with Penelope, even though they'd been together "officially" for more than three years at that point. To Amanda, Richard's affair with Penelope was still the greatest symbol that marriage could ultimately fail. She didn't like to think about that, especially not this close to her own wedding.

The ferry docked ten minutes after ten. Amanda

watched as her proud, confident, forty-something father strode down the ramp with beautiful Penelope beside him. Penelope had lost the baby weight completely and was just as leggy as she'd ever been. Amanda didn't like to think about how close in age they were.

"There she is. My darling daughter." Richard reached sold ground first and hugged Amanda, who, when she closed her eyes, allowed herself to dip into childhood memories. For so many years, she'd felt completely loved and protected by her father. "It's your wedding day!" Richard said as the hug broke. "Can you believe it?"

Amanda laughed. "Let's see if this one goes better than the last."

"It will," Richard assured her. "Sam is a tremendous young man."

After Richard stepped back, Penelope came forward with a perfumed hug and shrieked about how excited she was to see Amanda's wedding dress. "You did buy a new one, didn't you? You didn't decide to wear the old one..."

Amanda bristled at the question. *Who asked something like that?* "I have a new one," Amanda said, trying to be nice. "I think I like it even more than the last one. It suits me better."

Jake and Kristen came next, trying to wrangle their toddler and two five-year-old kids, who called Amanda's name and wrapped their arms around her legs. Jake hugged her from the side and said, "I hope you don't mind that I brought the whole circus with me?"

Just then, a car horn beeped from behind Amanda, and she whirled around to see Susan peering out of the front window of her car.

"Grandma!" The five-year-olds called her name and

hurried toward her, then leaped on her when she got out of the car. Susan was ecstatic.

"There you are, my little love bugs!" Susan knelt to hug both of them close, and Amanda allowed herself a moment of nostalgia and unbridled joy at the sight of her beautiful, youthful mother, who had taken to the grandmother role so easily.

Susan held her grandchildren's hands and guided them back to the rest of the family, where she hugged Jake and Kristen and greeted Richard and Penelope with happy eyes. She seemed unable to feel resentment toward them, not this deep into her own love story with Scott.

"Welcome back to Martha's Vineyard," she said. "Where are you staying?"

"We're at the Aquinnah," Richard explained. "Pen and I rented a swanky convertible for the occasion." He nodded toward the car rental area on the other side of the parking lot as Penelope raised her chin, clearly nervous in the middle of Richard's first family.

"Isn't that nice," Susan said. "We're staying at the Aquinnah tomorrow night, and that's it. Jake? Kristen? You guys ready to load up and come back with me?"

Kristen raised her fist excitedly, grateful to have a bit of help with the children. Amanda waved goodbye to Richard and Penelope, then helped Jake and Kristen with their suitcases and their children, then leaped into the back seat as Jake sat up front.

"Wow, it's busy," Jake said, commenting on the swarms of tourists around the docks, all dressed in summer dresses and linen pants and bright button-downs, many with hats on their heads.

"Tourist season is off to a brilliant start," Susan explained. "The Sunrise Cove is fully booked for the rest of the summer. Of course, much of that is due to Sam, my soon-to-be son-in-law, and his incredible abilities with social media."

"You must be glad you stopped your work at the hotel and returned to law," Kristen said.

Susan laughed. "We all help out at the Sunrise Cove when we can. But I have to admit. I wasn't made for hospitality, at least not full-time. My cousin Kelli just re-opened the Aquinnah Cliffside Overlook Hotel, where the wedding will be tomorrow, and I can tell she's up to her ears in worries and stress."

"I think she'll get through it with flying colors," Amanda said.

"I hope you're right," Susan said, her voice heavy with doubt.

"Uh oh. I know that tone," Jake teased their mother. "Mom's worried about the wedding!"

"I'm not," Susan said. "It's just that when we asked Kelli about having the wedding here, she said the hotel would be opened already in March or April. We figured that all the kinks of the place would be worked out by the time Amanda's wedding took place. Instead, it's only been six days since they opened the doors!"

"And have there been many problems?" Jake asked.

Susan shrugged. "I've hardly seen Kelli at all. She's just up there, working herself to death."

"It'll be fine, Mom," Amanda assured her. "As long as Sam is waiting for me on the other end of the aisle, I'll be happy."

Susan tried to laugh off her apprehension. "I can't shake that there's something off," she said as she pulled into her driveway. "But maybe my instincts are wrong."

In the rearview mirror, Jake locked eyes with

Amanda. They were accustomed to their mother's intuition, which they'd once set their clocks by. Then again, Susan hadn't known about Richard's affair for a long time after it had begun— so it wasn't like her intuition was completely foolproof.

After Susan cut the engine, Scott walked outside, waving as Susan's grandchildren burst from the car and began to run in circles around the yard. Kellan, his son, walked out behind him, a pair of binoculars from birdwatching across his chest.

"I always forget just how beautiful your new place is," Jake said, impressed as he followed Susan toward the back door, calling back for his children. Kristen came up behind him, their toddler in her arms.

As Jake and Kristen settled in for the weekend, Amanda said goodbye and headed back to the Sheridan House to rest up for the big night. Because the hotel was too chaotic and packed that evening, they'd opted against a proper rehearsal, but had arranged for a rehearsal dinner at the Sunrise Cove Inn Bistro. Those who had been invited would begin arriving around five-thirty, which gave Amanda about five hours to freak out, calm down, and freak out again, all on repeat.

Audrey and Grandpa Wes were out on the back porch of the Sheridan House, eating snacks and watching the water as Max played with his toy trucks on the floor.

"Did everyone make it to the island?" Grandpa Wes asked.

"Everyone is safe and accounted for," Amanda said. "Grandpa, I'm sure the kids want to see their great-grandfather."

Grandpa Wes burst to his feet with more energy than most men his age. "I'll see you ladies, later!" He then walked down the steps and took the path between their houses, whistling to himself.

Amanda took Grandpa Wes' place and crossed her arms, stirring with worry. She couldn't shake her mother's fears surrounding the wedding and her belief that something terrible was about to happen. But when she explained this to Audrey, Audrey just laughed.

"I love you and your mom to pieces, don't get me wrong, but you're both just anxious, busy bees," Audrey said. "If you don't have something to worry about, you don't know what to do with yourself."

Amanda groaned, knowing her cousin was right. "When will I outgrow that?"

"You're twenty-five now," Audrey said. "I hate to break it to you, but it's a part of you forever at this point. Better get used to it."

* * *

That night at five, Amanda met Sam in the foyer of the Sunrise Cove Inn. He was dressed wonderfully in a suit jacket and a button-up, and his cologne was sandalwood and leather, absolutely intoxicating as Amanda wrapped her arms around him. As they stood in the foyer, listening to the inn hum around them, Amanda was reminded of all those times after Sam had first started working at the Sunrise Cove, when Amanda had had to come up with excuse after excuse to see him there. It had always been the brightest time of her day.

"Sam?" Natalie, who had worked at the front desk of the hotel for many years, even before Susan had come back to the island, broke Amanda and Sam's reverie. "Can I ask you about something really quickly?"

"Natalie, it's their rehearsal dinner! Leave him be." This was Christine, who'd entered the foyer from the bistro, her dark hair streaming out behind her.

"It's not a problem," Sam assured her, stepping behind the counter to read an email Natalie needed help answering.

Amanda's heart swelled with love for him. He was the kind of man who was willing to go out of his way to ensure people were cared for.

Amanda and Christine entered the bistro, which had been completely reserved for Amanda's rehearsal dinner. The tables were decorated with white tablecloths, candles, and floral arrangements made by Claire herself. In the kitchen, Zach cooked up a tremendous bounty, grateful to contribute, yet again, to Amanda's party. Tomorrow, Chef Billiard would take the reins on the wedding reception itself, allowing even Zach to feast with the rest of them.

Very soon, family members began to arrive and fill out the tables, sitting where Amanda placed them with name cards. Amanda fell into a sort of frenzy, greeting Aunt Kerry and Uncle Trevor, cousin Andy and his wife, Beth, Jake, then Claire, then Lexi, then Rachel, then Everett, Charlotte's fiancé, who'd come to the wedding from his home on Orcas Island. Amanda faded in and out of consciousness as she said, "Thank you so much for coming!" and, "You look so beautiful!" and, "Yes, I'm so happy to be marrying Sam," over and over again, on a constant loop. She remembered reading once that brides forgot most of their wedding day due to adrenaline. She hoped she would find a way to slow down by tomorrow.

Just as the first appetizers arrived at the tables and guests began to eat and drink, Kelli and Xander appeared in the doorway to the bistro. Amanda leaped to her feet and cut across the restaurant to hug both of them.

"I can't believe you made it!" Amanda said.

Kelli grimaced. Her cheeks were slack. "We can't stay long."

Amanda frowned and nodded, remembering what her mother had said. "Is there something wrong?"

"Gosh. Just about everything," Kelli admitted.

"On the drive here, we got a call about an incident at the hotel," Xander explained.

"It's one incident after another, I'm afraid," Kelli said. "If anyone had told me how difficult this would be, I don't know that I would have made myself manager."

Amanda wavered on her feet, suddenly fearful for Kelli's mental health. She wanted to tell Kelli to step away from the role immediately to put herself first.

"After your wedding, I might re-evaluate," Kelli said. "But I want to make sure everything goes fluidly for you tomorrow."

"It'll be fine," Amanda said, squeezing Kelli's hand. "Why don't you grab something to eat on your way out? We have plenty of food."

Kelli's eyes glinted as Amanda waved over one of the servers, who carried a platter of salmon puffs. Kelli took one and ate it with her eyes closed, as though it was the most decadent thing she'd ever tasted.

"I could eat eighty more of those," Kelli admitted. "But I have to get back. Have a wonderful evening, won't you? Enjoy every second."

Amanda watched as Xander and Kelli made their way back into the evening, speaking to one another quietly before they leaped into Kelli's car and sped out of the parking lot. When Amanda turned back, she found her mother in front of her, watching her curiously.

"Why did Kelli run out like that?"

"There's an issue at the hotel," Amanda said timidly.

"Hmm." Susan wrinkled her nose. "I hope everything's okay?"

"It's all fine," Amanda assured her, waving her hand.

Just as Susan prepared to doubt her, Amanda turned as her father and Penelope entered the restaurant. Like always, Penelope wore high heels that rivaled some skyscrapers, and her father wore an immaculate suit. Susan turned and smiled at them genuinely, welcoming them to the bistro.

"Dad? Can I talk to you for a second?" Amanda sidled up alongside Richard, realizing this was her last chance to tell him about her decision for tomorrow.

"Of course. It's my honor to talk to the bride," Richard said, leaving Penelope on her own.

Amanda and Richard stepped off to the side of the growing crowd, where Amanda lowered her voice and said, "I just wanted to let you know about tomorrow."

"You want your mother to walk you down the aisle," Richard finished, his voice even.

Amanda's eyes widened. "How did you know?"

"Come on, hon. I'm no idiot." Richard's smile was nervous yet sincere. "For me, it's just a privilege to be involved in your life in some way after everything that happened."

Amanda swallowed the lump in her throat. Yet again, she struggled with questions surrounding Richard's decision to destroy their family, yet she drove them back into the dark recesses of her mind.

"Will you let me make a speech tonight instead?"

Richard asked, his voice breaking slightly. This was the only indication that he was in any way hurt by her decision.

"Of course," Amanda agreed. "That would be lovely."

After the appetizer course was finished and every single guest had been seated, champagne was uncorked and poured into flutes. Richard Harris then stood, his champagne lifted, and said, "I've been told I'm allowed to make a speech. If any of you know me, you know I'm a lawyer— like Amanda's mother, who is widely-known as the best defense attorney along the east coast, if not the country. I'm not the best. I'm not even the second-best. But I digress."

The guests laughed, falling easily into Richard's web. Susan's smile waned slightly as she took Scott's hand over the table, reminding him that he was her love, not Richard.

"I have had the unique privilege of watching Amanda grow up," Richard continued, his eyes focused upon Amanda's. "From the time she was a little girl, she was driven and focused, like her mother, but she also had a heart of gold and was always willing to slow down, look around her, and help someone in need. She's always had a unique balance, a wonderful sense of humility and humor, and a gorgeous way of looking at the world." Richard paused for a moment, then added, "Sam is the only young person I've ever met who could possibly fit into Amanda's world. Like Amanda, he's motivated and confident, but also like Amanda, he knows when to slow down, enjoy the moment, and, most notably for us here, fall in love. When Amanda first told me about him, she mentioned him as 'a friend,' but I think we all knew where they were headed. Maybe we knew before they did. I wish you both all the happiness in the world. I love you, honey."

Everyone in the bistro smiled knowing smiles, remembering watching Amanda and Sam circle one another for months before they admitted their love. Amanda wasn't sure whether to be embarrassed by that or grateful. More than anything, though, this was a small island with small-town gossip — and big-time love. She was just happy to be a part of all of it. She was happy to do it all with Sam by her side.

Chapter Ten

Xander and Kelli sped back to the Aquinnah Cliffside Overlook Hotel. Twice, Kelli tried to call Sandra, but both times, Sandra didn't answer and only texted back: "Just get here as soon as you can!"

"I couldn't understand what she said," Kelli confessed, her voice breaking. "She sounded so panicked."

"It'll be okay," Xander assured her.

The hotel was all lit up, looking immaculate and like a place lost in time, there at the edge of the cliffs. Xander parked the car, and together, they ran into the foyer to find Sandra at the front desk, white as a sheet. Before her, Miss Jennings, the older woman who couldn't stop complaining, looked irate. She waved her finger through the air, crying out as a crowd gathered around her. Behind her, her son held an unlit cigar and seemed to regard her as though she was a stand-up comedian.

"I don't think you know how important I am! Do you

understand anything I've told you? They're gone, and I want an explanation!" Miss Jennings said.

Terrified, Kelli placed a smile on her face and hurried forward. "Miss Jennings. Good evening. What seems to be the trouble?"

"There you are," Miss Jennings sniffed cruelly. "I've been looking all over for you. You know, you really need to keep your hotel in better working order."

"Should we speak in my office, Miss Jennings?" Kelli glanced nervously at the other guests, all of whom would probably post about this event on their social media channels.

"There is no reason to discuss this behind a closed door. This morning, I placed my earrings in my safe, and this evening, I opened the safe to find that they were gone. How on earth could that be, Miss Montgomery?" Miss Jennings demanded.

Kelli's stomach seized. Her first instinct was to tell Miss Jennings that she probably hadn't locked the safe correctly, that there was no way anyone could have broken into both her suite and her safe in one fell swoop. But then again, she hadn't learned anything about "blaming the customer" during her course in hotel management.

"Let's go to your suite, Miss Jennings," Kelli said, placing a gentle hand on Miss Jennings' upper arm and leading her to the elevator as Xander and Miss Jennings' son remained hot on their heels. In the elevator, nobody spoke, and Kelli stared at the numbers as they dinged from one to two to three, praying that this nightmare would be over soon. Perhaps Miss Jennings had misplaced the earrings in her room. Perhaps she'd never brought the earrings to the hotel at all.

When the elevator doors dinged open, Miss Jennings burst out and led them to her suite, where she opened the door and gestured toward the safe, which was now closed.

"I walked in to prepare for dinner, opened that thing, and found it empty!"

"Did you have anything else in the safe, Miss Jennings?"

"No," Miss Jennings snarled. "I didn't pack heavily this trip and never keep too much cash on me. For reasons exactly like this! You really can't trust anyone these days."

"You really can't," her son chimed in. He always seemed so eager to help.

"I think we had better call the police to make a statement," Xander said, choosing to play along with Miss Jennings' game. Kelli understood why. After all, Miss Jennings had the kind of power to ruin them.

"Miss Jennings, would you please open the safe for me? Just so we can make sure they're not in there somewhere," Kelli said.

Miss Jennings rolled her eyes thrice, then set to work unlocking the safe. When it was open, it shone back, clear and empty, without a single earring in sight. "Do you see what I mean?"

"It's not that I didn't believe you, Miss Jennings. It's just that I wanted to see it for myself before I called the police." Kelli nodded to Xander, who moved into the hallway to make the call. "Miss Jennings, I'm terribly sorry about this."

"It's been a horrible night," Miss Jennings went on with all the drama in the world. "I can't tell you how hard it's been for me. Those earrings were quite important to me. I got them in Milan with my third husband."

Kelli tried to maintain her smile, but it was difficult. It occurred to her that Miss Jennings had decided to make this up as a way to enliven her night at the hotel. Perhaps she was just a bored rich lady who wanted to make Kelli miserable.

"Tell me, Miss Montgomery. Why are you so wretched at managing this hotel?" Miss Jennings demanded.

Kelli swallowed a lump in her throat. "Miss Jennings, we are willing to do whatever we can to ensure your stay—"

"There's nothing you can do to save my trip now," Miss Jennings said. "It's all ruined!"

"Mother," her son said with a sigh. "At least get the room comped, for goodness' sake."

Kelli bristled, genuinely unsure what to say. If every rich woman like Miss Jennings decided to take advantage of the fledgling hotel, they wouldn't survive through the summer. Miss Jennings blinked at Kelli expectantly, and Kelli finally said, "Of course. We will be happy to comp tonight's stay."

At this, Miss Jennings leaned forward, her eyes in slits.

"I mean, we will comp all of your stay," Kelli said, flustered. "Unless we track down those earrings tonight, of course."

"I can't imagine why you wouldn't comp our entire stay," the son said, "if only because my mother has become very upset. This wouldn't have happened if you managed a better hotel."

Kelli nodded, her eyes filling with tears. Before she

started to sob in front of these horrible people, she stepped into the hallway and took several deep breaths, telling herself that this was just a bad night in the middle of a bad week, but that didn't mean it would turn out to be a bad summer and a bad year. Xander was finished with the police call, and he rubbed her shoulders and her back, murmuring, "These people are terrible. Your guests won't all be like that."

"I know you're right," Kelli said, although she wasn't sure right now. "What if she's making this up just to get a free stay?"

"There's nothing you can do," Xander whispered. "Just buckle down and stay strong. The police will be here soon, and when they're gone, we can go home and get some rest."

"I don't know. I feel like I can't leave the hotel tonight," Kelli said. "I left Sandra alone for like an hour, and this happened. I don't want to do that to her again."

Xander nodded. "Okay. But you have to promise me you'll start looking at applications for hotel managers by next week."

"I'll definitely fill Piper's position by next week," Kelli assured him. "But no matter what, I have a feeling this summer will be a difficult one."

"I'll be here for you," Xander said. "We can take a relaxing vacation this fall. Somewhere beautiful, warm, and foreign."

"You're speaking my language," Kelli said as she dropped her head on his chest, trying, yet failing to find excitement in such a far-off reality. She had to tackle tonight, Amanda's wedding, and the rest of the summer first. Then, she could think about relaxing.

It was nearly two that morning before the police left.

It took forever for Miss Jennings to give a report, a time that was only elongated by the ramblings of her son, who seemed quite drunk. Throughout, Kelli remained seated beside them, watching as Bobby, the police officer, scribbled notes to himself on his notepad.

Once the report was finished, Miss Jennings and her son flounced off, leaving Kelli with Bobby, who shrugged as he placed his paperwork back in his bag.

"What do you think, Bobby?" Kelli whispered. "Do you think Miss Jennings is telling the truth?"

"It's hard to say in these kinds of things," Bobby said. "If we hadn't taken Piper off your roster just yesterday, I'd have made the assumption that she was involved."

"You haven't arrested Piper yet, have you?"

"We're on the brink," Bobby explained as he walked toward the door, suppressing a yawn. "In the meantime, let me know if you have any more events like this. It's entirely possible that Piper gave out enough information about the hotel to her cohorts prior to her firing."

After he left, Kelli sat in the dark shadows of her office, staring into space as her heart thudded. Perhaps because she was a masochist, she pulled up social media again to look at photographs from Amanda's rehearsal dinner, where the faces of those she loved more than anything smiled, laughed, ate, and drank to their hearts' content, all in celebration of Amanda and Sam's young love.

"Nothing can go wrong tomorrow," Kelli said, mostly to her phone. "It will be perfect. It has to be."

Chapter Eleven

At two-thirty in the morning on the day of Amanda's wedding, Amanda woke up. For a moment, she wasn't sure where she was, a result of spending some nights in her home with Sam and other nights at the Sheridan House. Moonlight shimmered in from the window above her bed, making Audrey's face glow atop the second pillow, where she slept soundly. Amanda wasn't entirely surprised to see her. Her memories of last night's blissful rehearsal dinner ended at the Sheridan House, where she and Audrey had decided to have "just one more glass of wine" before they fell asleep. This had resulted in a very long conversation on Amanda's bed that had ended with both of them falling asleep. Such was the way of best friends.

"Tell me when you're going to have a baby," Audrey had begged Amanda last night. "I'll have another one so we can do it together."

Amanda's heart had seized at the thought. "Remember how nervous you were about having Max? You couldn't believe you were going to be a mother." She paused, then added, "Do you think you're ready to do it again?"

"I hardly remember life before Max," Audrey had said. "I was so naive, you know? I wanted to be a journalist in some sense, but I hardly even knew what that meant, either. I have this horrible memory of taking the pregnancy test when I was still at that internship in Chicago. When the two pink lines showed up, the entire nineteen years of my life flashed before my eyes."

"And then you came here."

"And then I came here." Audrey had taken another sip of wine and given Amanda a ponderous look. "But I'd love to do it all again with Noah. And to build our family here, in the Sheridan House? That's a dream come true."

Amanda had been quiet for a moment, imagining Audrey, Noah, Max, and their other children in that house, racing through time together.

Suddenly, Audrey said, "Promise that we'll always be there for each other. No matter what."

Amanda had laughed at such a silly promise. Her heart, mind, and spirit were forever linked to Audrey. "Audrey, you already know I'm here for you."

"Promise that you'll be here forever." This deep into the exhilarating and very drunk night, Audrey had looked on the verge of tears. "That no matter if our husbands leave us or our mothers die, you will always be here."

Amanda's throat had felt very tight. She'd wrapped her arms around Audrey and allowed herself to cry quietly, then whispered, "I promise."

It was true what Audrey said. There were no guarantees in life. More than that, their mothers were young and vibrant in many ways— but they were also older, the older

A Vineyard Love

generation, and eventually, they would leave Audrey and Amanda behind.

Now that Audrey was fast asleep in Amanda's bed, Amanda tip-toed to the window to peer at the moon overlooking the house. When she'd been a child, her father had told her about a man who'd lived on the moon, about how he knew if she'd done her chores or not. Although Amanda had been a very practical child, she hadn't been able to think of a reason why her father would lie to her about that.

Still, she'd always done her chores, no matter what, anyway. That was just her nature.

Although it was very late, Amanda hunted for her phone and sent a text message to Sam, who was staying at their home with his brother and a few of his friends. After the rehearsal dinner, Sam's friends had been slightly rowdy, singing songs and urging one another to take shots. Hilariously, most of the Montgomery and Sheridan men had gotten in on the fun, as well, including Steve, Andy, Uncle Trevor, and even Grandpa Wes. After he'd taken a shot of tequila, just as everyone had begun to wrap up for the night, Grandpa Wes had howled, "Oh boy! Let's get this party started!" His girlfriend, Beatrice, had shaken her head and said, "Let's head on home now." Everyone had waved Grandpa Wes out of the restaurant as though he were a hero.

To Amanda's surprise, Sam wrote back almost immediately.

> SAM: I can't sleep, either.
>
> SAM: I just keep thinking about how lucky I am to marry you tomorrow.

> SAM: If you'd told me I would have met someone as remarkable as you even three years ago, I would have said they were lying.

Amanda pressed her phone against her heart, wishing she could run through the inky black night to reach him. But just before she texted him another "goodnight," he wrote:

> SAM: Meet me outside!

Amanda wanted to protest— she wanted to tell him that they couldn't jinx the wedding. But she was too excited to see him, too excited to throw her arms around him and gaze at the stars together, so she put her tennis shoes on and hurried out into the darkness to see his car lights beaming down the road.

When Sam's car reached the driveway, Amanda leaped into the passenger seat. "Hi," she said, feeling like a teenager who'd snuck out— which was something Amanda Harris had never done, obviously, because she'd always had a test to study for or an early-morning practice to be rested for. Never had she been reckless until now.

"Hi." Sam laced his fingers through hers and beamed.

Enraptured, they kissed beneath the moonlight as the car buzzed beneath them, high on the certainty of their future. Sam turned off the engine, and they walked through the night, hand-in-hand, until they reached the Vineyard Sound. There, they removed their shoes and sat at the edge of the dock with their feet in the water, their chins lifted toward the stars.

"Do you think it's ridiculous that we couldn't wait till

later to see each other?" Amanda breathed, mostly to the stars.

"I think sometimes, when you know you want to spend your life with someone, it doesn't matter when that starts."

"So, we're starting the rest of our lives today at three o'clock in the morning?" Amanda laughed.

"Something like that." Sam kissed her cheek.

In the silence that followed, Amanda glanced back up at the beautiful Sheridan House, where her mother, Aunt Lola, and Aunt Christine had been raised by their parents, Grandpa Wes and Grandma Anna, until Anna's untimely death.

"In marrying you, I feel like we're becoming a part of the textured story of the Sheridan family," Amanda said.

"Especially because we're getting married in that haunted hotel," Sam said.

"Exactly." Amanda shivered, imagining what it had been like to be her Great-Grandma Marilyn all those years ago: in love with the stranger who owned the hotel, yet married to a terribly arrogant and selfish man named James. It boggled Amanda's mind to think of all the women throughout time who'd been married to men who'd treated them like second-class citizens. Sam would never do that.

"Thank you, by the way," Amanda said suddenly, surprising herself.

"For what?"

"For taking it slow when I needed it to be slow," Amanda breathed, "and for knowing when to speed it up when it was time."

Sam's smile widened. "For a little while, I thought

maybe I was wrong about you. I thought maybe you didn't care about me at all."

"Ha. You were literally all I thought about for months," Amanda remembered. "I made every excuse to come see you at the Sunrise Cove. I even learned to make your favorite sandwich just so I could bring it over to you."

"Reuben," Sam remembered. "That was the biggest sign of all that you were into me."

Amanda laughed, embarrassed at how obvious she'd been. "I was willing to make you hundreds of Reuben sandwiches, but I was never willing to tell you how I felt."

"Some people get caught in sandwich purgatory forever," Sam joked. "Luckily for us, we found a way out of that. And I still get plenty of Reubens out of you."

"Lucky for me, you learned my favorite sandwich, too," Amanda said gently.

"Goat cheese and plenty of green leaves," Sam said, wrinkling his nose. "My soon-to-be wife is a health nut. I reckon we'll live forever!"

Amanda laughed and cuddled him close. Before her, the moonlight flitted through the waves, the very top of a tremendous ocean, its depth impossible to know.

It was difficult to get Sam to leave, but eventually, Amanda confessed she needed one or two more hours of beauty sleep.

"Do you really want our guests to run out of the hotel screaming that they've seen a ghost?" Amanda said. "It won't be the ghost of Great-Grandma Marilyn. It'll be me, very sleepy Amanda."

When Amanda returned to her bedroom, Audrey half-opened her eyes, watching as Amanda slid under the covers again.

"You two are obsessed with each other," Audrey said sleepily. "I heard you down by the water, laughing like teenagers."

"You and Noah are the same way," Amanda told her, her heart very full as she drifted back to sleep.

Never one to sleep in, Amanda managed to rise by six-thirty to go for a run, shower, and make herself a green smoothie, all before Audrey and Max got up. Max babbled happily in his highchair as Audrey sipped her coffee, her eyes glazed.

"It's too bad Grandpa can't be here for your last morning home," Audrey said, eyeing the boxes in the corner of the living room, which Noah had brought over yesterday. "Tomorrow, when Noah moves in, everything will be different."

As though he'd heard her, Grandpa Wes suddenly barrelled through the back door of the Sheridan House, calling out, "Honey! I'm home!" as though he were a sitcom character.

Audrey and Amanda popped up, watching as he emerged from the shadows of the mudroom, wearing a devilish grin.

"Grandpa!" Amanda hugged him first. "We didn't think you'd make it."

"I told Beatrice to drive me," Wes explained. "I couldn't miss your last morning, Mandy." He dropped back from their hug and placed his hands on her shoulders. "I'm just so dang proud of the young woman you've grown into."

With tears in her eyes, and for the very last time as a single woman, Amanda prepared breakfast for all of them, which included eggs for healthy protein, whole-grain toast, vegetarian sausages, avocados, and fresh berries. As the veggie sausages sizzled, Audrey helped Grandpa Wes with the crossword, pondering quietly as Grandpa Wes pointed out a bird in the window. "I haven't seen a Great Auk like that in years. Look at the wings on him!"

Amanda could have wept, but she didn't want to ruin the mood. So, she plated everyone's breakfast, put on the radio, and sat with three of her favorite people in the world, preparing her heart and mind for the next phase of her life. It was just as her mother had always said: it was best to start the day with breakfast. After that, you had the strength for whatever life threw at you.

Chapter Twelve

Kelli awoke to the sound of Xander's voice. Still groggy, she kept her eyes closed, listening as Xander said, "Hello, baby. Good morning," and then kissed her on the cheek, on the forehead, and on the lips. It took a moment for Kelli to realize she wasn't safely tucked into bed beside him, that she was, in fact, still in her clothes from last night, her face caked with makeup, and her mind wild with stress. She felt nauseated. Her eyes popped open.

"Xander!" She rose up from the couch in her office and rubbed her eyes, feeling defeated.

Xander was, as usual, dressed immaculately in an Italian-cut suit and Italian suede shoes, and his cologne was sandalwood and leather and something else, maybe vanilla. Kelli could have basked in how handsome he was all day. Then again, she had a to-do list about a mile long, and, according to the clock on the wall, it was already nine.

"I can't believe I slept here," she said, trying to laugh it off.

"I kept waking up at home, looking for you," Xander said. "I called a few times, but you must have slept through the rings."

Kelli glanced at her phone, which was filled with missed calls from Xander. "I figured if I stayed the night, I could wake up early and jumpstart on everything I need to do today. So much for that."

"Let me order you some breakfast." Xander turned and grabbed a mug of coffee from the desk, which he passed to her now.

"You're an angel," Kelli breathed, taking the coffee. It was hazelnut and warm, and it immediately animated a few of her dead brain cells.

With Xander downstairs ordering the breakfast, Kelli changed into another work dress, sprayed her hair with dry shampoo, and redid her makeup. She then checked on the status of the vendors who were delivering goods for Amanda's wedding that morning and early afternoon to ensure they would make it in time. According to the website that listed mailing information, all of the vendors were either on their way or had already dropped off supplies.

Xander returned with breakfast bagels piled with egg, cheese, and bacon and two more coffees.

"There's a bit of drama in the kitchen right now," Xander said, as though he wasn't sure he wanted to confess this to Kelli before she ate.

Kelli groaned. "What's up?"

"All these vendors are arriving."

"For Amanda's wedding."

"Right. But it seems like their stuff is getting in the way of Chef Billiard's stuff, and some of the kitchen staff

A Vineyard Love

are being really unkind to the delivery drivers," Xander explained.

Kelli took a big bite of her bagel sandwich, already knowing she wouldn't have time to eat the entire thing before she had to run downstairs to put out the first fire of the day.

"Next week," Kelli assured Xander, as though she could read his mind. "I promise that I'll find someone to take over."

After Kelli ate one-half of her breakfast bagel, she and Xander hurried downstairs, where they parted ways. Xander had a meeting with a business associate that morning, which he'd planned to have right there in the ballroom. Meanwhile, Kelli passed by Sandra on the way to the kitchen, who smiled nervously.

"Are you holding up okay, Sandra?" Kelli asked.

"I'm holding on for dear life!" Sandra joked.

"Big wedding today," Kelli said.

"We can get through this," Sandra assured her. "Let me know any way that I can support you."

"Just keep doing what you're doing," Kelli said as she breezed past, then shot through the kitchen door to discover a chaotic scene.

Three of Chef Billiard's kitchen staffers, guys in their twenties who'd come to the hotel specifically to work under such a renowned chef, stood around boxes and carts that had been piled high with supplies for Amanda's wedding. It seemed that, instead of finding a place to put the supplies, they'd decided to stand around, complaining about it. Their endless complaints meant that the rest of the kitchen was behind on breakfast orders. Just before Kelli interrupted their endless barrage of annoyances, one of the servers burst into the kitchen and said, "We have seven tables who've been waiting for their breakfast for over an hour. Don't you know I work for tips?"

"If you want to do real work, come back here!" one of the kitchen staffers blared at the server. "We can trade places."

"Right. I'm sure you'll wow the tables with that charm," the server said, crossing her arms over her chest.

Nobody had noticed Kelli was there, watching them, aghast. It seemed she'd lost total control over the hotel.

"Everyone!" Kelli clapped her hands to get their attention.

At this, the feuding kitchen staffers, the sous chefs, and the server turned and glared at Kelli, as though she was the reason for all this drama.

"Let's get this worked out," Kelli said. "We have an extra walk-in fridge for a reason, guys. Put the wedding stuff in there— get it out of the way. And get back to work!"

After a dramatic pause, the staffers kicked themselves into gear and began to carry the boxes to the back fridge.

"Give the tables free mimosas," Kelli instructed the server as sweat billowed up on her neck. "Tell them we have a wedding today and that things are chaotic. People love talking about weddings."

"Okay." The server brightened slightly, knowing that free alcohol always equated to happier tables. She sped off to tend to them, which left Kelli to collapse against the counter. As soon as the boxes were cleared and the staffers returned to their post, she thanked them and hurried back to the front desk, where Sandra greeted everyone with a big smile.

"I put out the kitchen fire," Kelli told Sandra between guest visits, scrubbing her fingers through her messy hair.

"Great work, boss," Sandra said.

"Now, just another twenty-four hours till I can sleep," Kelli joked.

As Sandra chuckled, a woman in her sixties approached the front desk. She wore a black beaded dress and a big hat, as though nobody had alerted her it was nearly summer, and her eyebrows were cinched tightly together, producing thick wrinkles up her forehead.

"Good morning," Kelli said. "My name is Kelli. I'm the manager here at the hotel. Can I help you with something?"

"Hello." The woman spoke very quietly, which forced Kelli to lean far over the counter to hear her. "I've probably made a mistake. I don't know."

"What seems to be the problem?" Kelli asked, with a slight twinge of annoyance in her voice.

"I've looked all over my room," the woman said, lacing her fingers together. "In the safe. Under the bed. Between the sheets. But my rings, they're gone. And honey..." The woman leaned so close that her nose nearly touched Kelli's. "Those rings were worth more than you make in a year."

Kelli immediately resented the fact that this woman had any hunch of what Kelli made. There was a strange, evil glint in her eyes, one that made Kelli question if she wanted to help her at all. But the customer was always right, or at least Kelli had to believe that in order to keep the hotel afloat.

"You've looked everywhere?" Kelli repeated.

"Absolutely everywhere."

Kelli sighed and dropped the woman's gaze. A thought struck her: maybe Miss Jennings had told this woman that her room had been comped due to the "thieving" of her earrings, which had given this woman the idea. Kelli's head spun. Her hotel would never make it if she continued to comp very expensive rooms. She imagined a horrible future, wherein people came to the hotel, pretended to have their things stolen, and then enjoyed the fruits of comped rooms into infinity. *What was she going to do?*

"We should really call the police," Kelli heard herself say because she wasn't sure what else to do.

The woman studied Kelli sternly, as though she didn't trust her at all. Kelli wasn't sure she trusted herself, either.

But just as Kelli reached for the phone to call Officer Bobby back to the hotel for another round, two beautiful and familiar faces entered the lobby.

Susan Sheridan and Amanda Harris smiled eagerly, bustling through the sunbeams of the ornate foyer, both effervescent with excitement for the approaching wedding. Amanda carried her bagged dress easily and walked with her shoulders back, entering the day that would change her life forever with poise and confidence.

Horribly, Kelli cursed their entrance. She didn't want Susan to know just how little control she had over the hotel, especially not today of all days. Kelli braced herself with a smile. "Amanda! Susan! Happy wedding day!" She then quickly whispered to Sandra to say, "Can you call the police? Try to get Officer Bobby. He was so understanding the other night."

"I'm on it," Sandra assured her, smiling as she took over.

This left Kelli to breeze around the side of the desk and swallow first Amanda, then Susan in hugs. Both of them smelled wonderful, like the sea and like lavender, and Kelli hoped they couldn't sense that she hadn't showered and had spent the night on a couch.

"I can't believe it's here," Amanda said of the day, adjusting her dress on her arm.

"The suite is all ready for you," Kelli said, guiding them to the grand staircase, up the steps, and into the room they'd reserved for Amanda, Susan, Christine, Lola, Audrey, and two of Amanda's friends from Newark.

"The hairdressers will be here soon," Amanda explained as she spread her dress across a cream couch.

"Wonderful," Kelli said. "In the fridge, I've set aside several bottles of champagne for you. I'll have the servers bring up some hors d'oeuvres as well. You know the number-one rule for brides."

"Don't fall?" Amanda joked.

Kelli laughed, although she was too stressed to really find anything funny right now. "Brides always forget to eat. Keep yourself fed today. We need you up at the altar!"

"If you say so," Amanda said.

Kelli breezed back out of the suite, then leaned against the wall, out of sight, and took several deep breaths. As she waited for herself to stabilize, she listened to Susan and Amanda in the next room, talking about how beautiful the suite was and how marvelous the day had gone so far. All Kelli had to do was maintain their level of happiness.

"Kelli?" Christine and Lola appeared on the staircase in front of her, smiling Sheridan-women smiles.

Kelli burst away from the wall. They'd caught her taking a moment to herself, which shouldn't have been allowed on such a dramatic day.

"Happy wedding day!" Kelli cried, her voice nearly

breaking. "Susan and Amanda are already in the suite. There's plenty of champagne to go around."

"Won't you have a glass with us?" Lola asked.

Kelli winced, watching as, far down the staircase, Officer Bobby returned to the hotel, in-uniform, then strode up to the front desk to speak with the woman whose rings were supposedly "nowhere to be found."

"I have to run, unfortunately," Kelli said. "Have an extra glass for me, won't you?" She then fled down the staircase, her heart in her throat, praying that very soon, she would find time to sit down again.

Chapter Thirteen

For the wedding, Amanda had purchased herself, her bridesmaids, and her mother and aunts beautiful silk robes with their initials monogrammed on the left chest. Now that Christine and Lola had arrived, Amanda slid the robes from the bag her mother had carried in and passed them out, saying, "I want us to be cozy before we have to put our dresses on."

"Amanda! These are divine!" Lola cried as she raised the robe in front of her.

Already, Christine unbuttoned her blue dress and slipped into the robe, saying, "That fabric is such a relief."

"So luxurious," Susan agreed as she swung her arms through hers and flipped her hair out along her shoulders. "It was such a good idea, Amanda."

"What was a good idea?" Audrey appeared in the doorway, wearing a mischievous smile. Although Amanda had just said goodbye to her at the Sheridan House only twenty minutes ago, Audrey raced across the suite to throw her arms around Amanda. "The robes! You really got them?" She quickly changed, throwing all modesty out the window, and looked at herself in the floor-to-ceiling mirror along the wall, which offered three different angles so you could see that much more of yourself. "I want to walk down the aisle in this. Can I?"

Amanda laughed. "I only spent months picking out the perfect bridesmaid dresses..."

"You probably spent months picking out the perfect robes, too," Audrey pointed out.

Susan grimaced, looking slightly uneasy, as though she wasn't entirely sure if Audrey was joking or not. Amanda knew her mother was anxious about the wedding, wanting everything to go precisely to plan— all because of her love for Amanda. Amanda knew better than most that tremendous love often meant tremendous fear.

"She's just being Audrey," Lola told Susan, placing her hand on Susan's shoulder.

"I know. I know." Susan tried to laugh, but it sounded all wrong.

Christine opened the fridge to find a bottle of champagne, which she opened with ease, without making it pop, which was proof of her many years in the gastronomy business. She then poured five glasses, which they all raised. The bubbles glinted in the sunlight.

"We made it," Susan breathed, her eyes a mix of sorrow and unadulterated joy. "My little girl is getting married today. I just love you so much, Amanda. I don't know what to say."

This was a rarity. Susan Sheridan always knew what to say.

"I'll say something," Audrey said, raising her glass a little bit more. "I don't know if I've ever been happier to watch someone else's love story play out. Sam and

Amanda remind me that true love exists— but that it's different than I ever imagined it to be. It takes work. It takes compromises. And more than anything, it requires a very good sense of humor. I mean, just this morning, at three, in fact, it sounded like there were a couple of teenagers down by the water."

"Audrey!" Amanda cried.

"You were out with Sam this morning?" Lola's smile was mischievous, just like Audrey's.

Amanda's cheeks burned with embarrassment.

"You just couldn't wait to see each other?" Lola continued.

Susan grimaced, as though fearful.

"I don't believe in all that bad luck stuff anymore," Amanda told her mother with a shrug. "I genuinely trust Sam. I know he'll be there for me."

It took Susan a split-second to fix her face. "I trust Sam, too, of course. I'm just surprised you didn't want to get a full night of sleep. That's all."

"She was too excited," Christine pointed out. "I understand that all too well."

"Let's just relax, drink some champagne, and enjoy this day," Amanda said. "I'm so glad all of you are here to support me. I don't know what I would have done without you these past few years. You've been my rock."

Silence fell over the group as they drank. For a moment, everyone seemed too emotional to speak. But Audrey, never one to allow a dull second to pass, jumped to action, setting up a speaker to play some of her and Amanda's favorite tunes. "What a Girl Wants" by Christina Aguilera played first, and Audrey picked up her hairbrush and began to sing with her eyes closed. She was nowhere close to hitting Christina's notes.

"Is this the bride's suite?" A woman with bright green hair peeked her head through the door.

Amanda laughed and waved her in. "Jamey! Hi! Welcome!"

Jamey was the hairstylist Amanda had decided on for the wedding. Jamey had brought two of her hairstylist friends, Connie and Barbara, who followed into the suite after her and began to set themselves up along the long desk of the room. Their bags were stuffed with supplies like hair rollers, hairspray, gel, creams, hair straighteners, hot curlers, and other stuff Amanda couldn't identify. They'd also brought with them a cloud of scents, as though wherever they went, they brought the smell of the salon with them.

"Amanda, let's get started," Jamey ordered, pointing at a chair. "We don't have as long as you'd think."

Amanda hopped toward Jamey, where she set her champagne flute on the desk. Jamey whipped a black bib around her entire body, then set to work on what they'd agreed on: a half-up, half-down 'do with gorgeous, shining curls and bangs. Because Amanda's hair had gotten unruly in the bang department, Jamey spritzed her hair with water and gave Amanda a trim. Amanda watched her dark curls cascade to the ground.

"We saw Kelli on the way up here," Christine said, refilling her and Lola's champagne flutes. "She looked super stressed."

Lola nodded. "I thought she was about to burst into tears."

Susan made a face. "I hope she's not in over her head."

"Did you hear about her second-in-command?" Audrey said, in full gossip-mode.

"No? What happened?" Susan asked.

"Apparently, she had to fire her," Audrey said. "The cops came and said they'd learned she was part of a big ring of island thieves."

"Island thieves?" Susan's jaw dropped. "I haven't heard anything about that. And you would have thought I'd have at least a few of them as clients."

Audrey shrugged. "I don't think they've caught many of them yet. Kelli's second-in-command was the tip of the iceberg. They're hoping Piper will clue them in on who else is involved."

"Goodness," Amanda breathed.

"Anyway. I think that's why Kelli is running around so frantically. She's lost a big part of her staff, and she's not sure how to proceed," Audrey said.

"Too bad the groom is a hotel manager as well," Christine said. "If he wasn't so busy with other tasks today, he might be able to help out."

"Don't let Sam know that," Amanda said. "He's too helpful. He'll miss half the wedding, just trying to keep Kelli above water."

Everyone laughed, knowing the goodness of Sam's heart. Lola sipped her champagne and nearly spat it up again, saying, "Sorry. I'm just imagining Sam in his perfect tuxedo behind the hotel's front desk, saying, 'One more minute, Amanda! I'll be right there!' As you're waiting to cut the cake."

Amanda threw her head back with laughter, and Jamey swatted her. "Hey! I'm in the middle of giving you a bridal look!"

"Sorry!" Amanda winced and straightened her head.

Very soon after, Amanda's two best friends from Newark, Brittany and Brooke, arrived. They were enthusiastic, breaking out another bottle of champagne and gossiping with Amanda about the other friends Amanda had invited to the wedding, all of whom they'd been friends with back in her old life. It was still bizarre for Amanda to think of these people as parts of her past. All of them had known Amanda to be Chris' long-term girlfriend— all of them had been at the last wedding and witnessed her defeat.

Still, she knew they were happy for her. She knew they were cheering her on.

Around one, guests for the wedding began to arrive at the Aquinnah Cliffside Overlook Hotel for one and a half hours of a cocktail and hors d'oeuvre pre-wedding meet-and-greet. It was a glorious seventy-five-degree day, and guests spilled out across the veranda and the lush grounds, sipping cocktails and glasses of wine as a Vineyard sunlight burst in and out of fluffy, cartoon clouds. From the top of the staircase, Amanda, who was in curlers and halfway-done makeup, peered down at her guests, watching as they laughed and chatted, all in luxurious summertime clothes— dresses and suits and even hats, women's jewelry glinting from necks and wrists and ears. It blew Amanda away that so many people saw her wedding as a time to see and be seen. It was one of the social events of the summer, and it wasn't even summer yet.

"Are you spying?" Audrey sidled up to her, her hair also raised in curlers and her champagne flute in her hand.

"Something like that."

"Once the day starts, these people won't be able to get enough of you," Audrey reminded her. "Just an hour or two till showtime."

Amanda winced. A part of her wanted to run down the hallway to the groomsmen's suite just to ensure Sam was still on the property. She wanted him to be right there beside her, reminding her he wouldn't ever leave her alone. *Why was she still so insecure?*

"Look! Isn't that Officer Bobby?" Audrey pointed down at the crowd, where an officer strode alongside Kelli. Kelli's face was pained, and she spoke directly into Officer Bobby's ear, as though she didn't want anyone else to hear what she said.

"Poor Kelli," Amanda breathed. "Remind me never to operate a hotel."

"Does Sam have this much trouble?"

"The Sunrise Cove has been around for so long that it sort-of runs itself," Amanda said. "And I have a hunch that the Aquinnah Cliffside's elegant guests don't make it easy on Kelli."

Kelli and the officer stood at the front door for a long time. Officer Bobby touched his walkie-talkie as Kelli crossed and uncrossed her arms. As she stood there, her father, Uncle Trevor, and her mother, Aunt Kerry, breezed past, hugging and kissing her. Kelli fixed her face immediately, clearly wanting to show just how happy and with-it she was. Amanda's heart went out to her. She understood what it was like to pretend. It was exhausting.

Chapter Fourteen

"I can't afford to comp every room, Bobby," Kelli muttered under her breath as the officer prepared to leave. He'd taken a police report from the woman with the supposedly stolen rings, who'd said they were worth one-hundred and fifty thousand dollars.

"I know that," Officer Bobby told her. "But that woman's threats were terrifying. She could take down the hotel. Easy."

Kelli grimaced. "I never imagined I'd be at the mercy of so many terrible rich people."

"It's just the first week's kinks," Bobby told her. "We're all pulling for you down at the station. Let us know how we can help."

"Can you babysit some of the women at this hotel to make sure they don't misplace their jewelry?"

"I'm not sure about that," Bobby said with a laugh. "Although I wish I could."

Kelli watched Officer Bobby go, teetering nervously from one heel to the other. Her mouth felt strange and tangy, and she was terribly hungry, as the one-half of the bagel sandwich hadn't gotten her very far. Already, guests for Amanda's wedding had begun to celebrate, and they crowded through the ballroom and out along the veranda and the grounds. Their conversations were soothing, a dull roar of laughter, stories, and compliments. Because she'd said hello to her parents only briefly, she beelined for them and put on the very brightest smile she could muster.

"Mom! Dad! Sorry I couldn't chat earlier. I see you've already gotten some drinks?"

Kelli's mother raised her vodka tonic. "The bartender is quite good."

"She just has a crush on him," Trevor teased.

"I do. Perhaps a bit." Kerry wagged her eyebrows playfully as Trevor kissed her gently on the cheek.

"What do you think of the party so far?" Kelli asked her parents.

"It's beautiful, honey," Kerry said. "You should really get a drink and enjoy it for a little while."

Kelli glanced back at the front desk, which was empty save for Sandra, who scribbled something down on a notepad as though it was the most important thing on earth.

Suddenly, out of nowhere, Xander appeared through the crowd, carrying a Negroni and an Aperol Spritz. His eyes glinted with good humor.

"There's your handsome fiancé!" Kerry teased.

"I can't believe I caught you standing in one place," Xander teased as he passed her the Aperol Spritz, her favorite drink.

"I shouldn't drink this," Kelli said hesitantly, considering the mess in the kitchen, the mess of her guests, and the mess of her to-do list.

"Just one drink won't hurt," Xander assured her.

"You have to learn how to manage stress," Kerry said. "When your father and I were at the top of our game in real estate, we had to force ourselves to take vacations and days off. But our career was better for it."

"Yes, but Mom, this is the first week of the hotel being open. There are still so many things to figure out," Kelli tried.

"Even so," Kerry said. As Kelli's mother, Kelli's health would always come first for her, not the bottom line of the hotel. Kelli had to appreciate that.

"There she is!" Suddenly, Kelli's Uncle Wes appeared alongside his beautiful girlfriend, Beatrice, who wore a beaded blue dress and sensible heels. "Beatrice, isn't my niece a genius? This entire hotel was her vision."

Kelli blushed and waved her hand.

"It's true," Kerry reminded her. "Remember all those nights you spent at our house, telling me about your ideas for this very ballroom? You had a whole list of artists you wanted to feature. Local artists you wanted to uphold."

Kelli remembered that long-ago day when the day-to-day logistics of the hotel hadn't been a problem and she'd been allowed to revel in beautiful things.

"Show us some of that art!" Uncle Wes cried.

Kelli sipped her Aperol Spritz, allowing her anxious thoughts to slow. "Okay. Well. Up there, over the bar, is a beautiful take on Art Deco, but done by a wonderful Nantucket painter."

"Oh! The other island," Uncle Wes joked.

"Don't worry. I have plenty of Martha's Vineyard artists around here," Kelli said, surprised that her smile felt natural. "There's a great one in the lobby, actually. Let me show you."

Kelli led her mother, her father, her fiancé, her uncle, and Beatrice into the foyer, where she hoped to show them "Vineyard Starlight," a transcendent painting a Martha's Vineyard artist had painted of the lighthouse at night. But when Kelli reached the floor directly beneath where she'd had the painting hung (an event she'd been present for), she gaped up at a wall that was now completely empty.

For a moment, her family was quiet behind her, clearly waiting for her to say something. *But what could she say?*

"Um. The painting was right here?" Kelli muttered as she turned back to lock eyes with her mother.

Kerry frowned. "Have your decorators moved things around on you?"

"Nobody was told to make any adjustments to the paintings," Kelli said firmly.

Xander suddenly looked very pale. "Kelli..." he began.

"There has to be an explanation," Kelli said. It suddenly felt as though the ground beneath her feet was uneven. "I mean, maybe they got some bad information. Or maybe the painting was damaged? Or?"

Kelli's mother and father exchanged worried glances. In the strange silence, Xander stepped forward to take Kelli's arm gently. "We'd better check on that together. Right, Kelli?"

"When you find it, I'd love to see it," Uncle Wes said brightly, trying to soothe Kelli's fears.

"Of course. You four will be the first people to see it once it's back in place," Kelli assured them. "Go back to the ballroom! Enjoy the party. The hors d'oeuvres are to die for. I didn't hire one of the best chefs on the eastern seaboard for nothing."

"Don't tell that to Zach!" Uncle Wes joked, speaking of Christine's husband.

Kelli feigned laughter until she and Xander turned the corner and stalled in the back hallway. Kelli felt out of breath. Just before she could speak, however, her phone buzzed with a text from Charlotte, her sister.

> CHARLOTTE: Hey, sis!
>
> CHARLOTTE: Happy wedding day.
>
> CHARLOTTE: I'm in the kitchen of the hotel, looking for the big order of champagne. It should have been delivered this morning around ten-thirty. Any chance you know where it ended up?

> KELLI: It's got to be in the extra walk-in fridge in the back.
>
> KELLI: The kitchen staffers were annoyed at all the space the wedding stuff was taking up, so I told them to put everything back there.

> CHARLOTTE: A lot of that stuff is in there, yeah. But not the champagne.
>
> CHARLOTTE: It should have been five crates' worth.

Kelli closed her eyes, annoyance and fear rolling through her.

"What's going on?" Xander asked.

"Apparently, Charlotte can't find the champagne. And it's not where I told the kitchen staff to put it."

"I can head back to the kitchen to help her find it," Xander said.

Charlotte sputtered. "That's not even the biggest problem right now! Where is that painting? Xander, it's worth so much money. Like, more than all the other paintings on the wall of that room combined."

Xander winced.

"Is it possible that someone stole it?" Kelli demanded, her voice very low.

"I don't think we should jump to any conclusions," Xander said.

But Kelli's head was whirring with images of Miss Jennings, of the woman with the stolen rings, and now, of the empty space on the wall where the painting should have been. Something was going on. Although her gut was often wrong (she had married Mike, for crying out loud), it now felt so terrible that she couldn't ignore it.

Again, Charlotte's text came in rapid succession.

> CHARLOTTE: Help! We need more champagne!

Kelli groaned as Xander tried to calm her.

"Let's go to the kitchen. After that, we can head to the security room," Xander reminded her.

"Right! We can check the CCTV footage to see when the painting was moved," Kelli said. Overwhelmed with emotion, she tore forward and kissed Xander with her eyes closed, so grateful for his help. "You are a brilliant, brilliant man."

Xander laughed. "I'm not brilliant in the slightest. This hotel management stuff is a whole lot harder than it looks."

"Add an art heist to the mix, and things get complicated," Kelli agreed.

Together, Kelli and Xander hurried back to the

kitchen, where they found Charlotte in a similar state of stress. She hovered over ten boxes, all of which she'd torn open, on the hunt for the champagne. She also spoke quickly into her walkie-talkie as she worked, trying her best to sound chipper even as she fell apart.

"Hi!" Charlotte's eyes were enormous.

"No luck?" Kelli asked.

Charlotte's shoulders fell forward. "I don't have any idea what to do."

"We have plenty of white wine and beer," Kelli reminded her. "Maybe I can call another hotel here on the island and see if they can lend us some champagne."

"It won't be enough," Charlotte said. "And you know as well as I do that all of the hotels on the island have weddings today. It's a gorgeous Saturday in June! It's prime real estate for weddings!"

Kelli took a step back, away from Charlotte's volatility. Although she adored her little sister, there was nothing she could do for her right then.

"Listen," Kelli said. "There's some weird stuff going on here at the hotel. Have you seen anyone around? Anyone who looks suspicious?"

Charlotte gaped at her. "All I can do right now is keep myself, the bride, and the bride's mother afloat."

"Of course. Of course!" Kelli tried to laugh it off, but sensed there was nothing she could say to get Charlotte back on track. But as she stirred in the silence, Chef Billiard stormed into the kitchen in his chef whites and cried out, "Where on earth is my knife?"

What now? Kelli stared at Chef Billiard, whose cheeks were beefy red with anger. Instead of projecting his anger toward her, however, he began to scream at all of the members of the kitchen staff, accusing them of misplacing his perfect Japanese knife.

"I cannot, under any circumstances, produce this wedding dinner without that knife!" Chef Billiard blared. "What was the first rule I told each and every one of you during your very first shift with me?"

When silence proceeded his question, Chef Billiard's face got, impossibly, even redder. "I don't hear you! What was the first rule I taught you?"

"Never touch your knife!" one of the kitchen staffers cried, his voice wavering.

"That's right. Never, under any circumstances, touch my knife. Now, it seems that one of you has gone out of your way to disobey me."

Kelli's stomach twisted with fear. Stuttering, she said, "Chef Billiard, the wedding dinner is set for five. I don't suppose you could make an exception, just this once, to work with another knife?"

But Chef Billiard flat-out ignored her and continued to storm through his kitchen, enraged. Meanwhile, servers came and went, bent on delivering the beautiful hors d'oeuvres to Amanda's guests.

"Come on," Xander muttered into Kelli's ear. "We can check on this storm in a little while. Let's look at the CCTV footage."

Kelli nodded, grateful he'd decided to take the lead. Without him, she would have drowned.

Chapter Fifteen

Kelli and Xander burst from the kitchen and found themselves at the outer reaches of Amanda's pre-wedding cocktail party. Kelli immediately fixed her face, smiling at her sister, Claire, who drank a cocktail and chatted with her daughters, Gail and Abby, and her niece, Rachel, who had a headset on and was presumably helping Charlotte with the wedding festivities.

"How are you doing?" Kelli asked as they breezed past.

"It's a gorgeous wedding," Claire said. "Has Charlotte tracked down that champagne yet?"

"I think she's nearly there," Kelli lied.

"Wonderful!" Claire said.

Kelli and Xander sped up, driving through the crowd. Once they reached the other side, they took the staircase to the third floor, where Kelli used her master key to open the security room. There, several TVs presented black-and-white images of various areas of the hotel: the foyer, the kitchen, several hallways, the ballroom, and the exterior. Kelli hadn't gotten around to hiring someone to watch the televisions every day. She just hadn't assumed the Aquinnah Cliffside would become one of those hotels that needed it. How wrong she'd been!

In the current image of the foyer, the wall held no painting.

"Can we rewind that particular video?" Kelli asked. "From what I remember, the painting was still there last night. I swear I talked about it with someone. Maybe a guest?"

"Of course." Xander sat in front of the controls and began to press buttons that meant absolutely nothing to Kelli. But even when he rewound to yesterday, then three days before, then over a week ago— prior to the opening of the hotel itself, the spot on the wall remained empty, as though the painting had never existed.

"Weird," Xander muttered.

"I know for a fact the painting was there over a week ago," Kelli insisted. "It was only hung a few days before the opening party!"

"I watched you and the designer handling it," Xander told her. "But that means someone has tampered with the security footage."

"No..." Kelli breathed. "I mean, who would do that?"

"Someone wanted to hide that they'd taken the painting. They've somehow tapped into the system to play the same footage on a loop rather than showing any video footage where the painting was there. I guess it's a form of gaslighting. It's sort of genius."

"What about the other footage?" Kelli demanded. "What about the kitchen?" She noted in the current video that the chef's knife was not located in its normal spot.

"Let's check." Xander tried to erase the footage all the

way back to yesterday, but the footage remained similar, on a loop.

"There's no way the knife wasn't there yesterday," Kelli said. "Chef Billiard always puts it exactly in the same place. And he must have used it this morning!"

To check, Kelli texted Charlotte.

> KELLI: Hey! Can you ask Chef Billiard if he had his knife this morning?

> CHARLOTTE: No can do. I'm in panic-mode, trying to find these champagne crates. I don't have time to track down some psychopath's knife.

Kelli closed her eyes, feeling suddenly as though she and Charlotte were teenagers, squabbling about something at home rather than two grown adults trying to keep their businesses afloat. She wanted to write back: *thanks for nothing*, but she stopped herself. Charlotte was stressed.

"I mean, there's no way that a painting of that size got out of the hotel without someone seeing it," Kelli said suddenly.

Xander nodded. "Someone must have seen it being moved, at least."

"We should ask the staff. Even the guests, as long as we find a way to word it that doesn't frighten them."

"Let's do it," Xander said.

Downstairs, Kelli found Sandra behind the front desk, helping a twenty-something who was on her honeymoon with recommendations for places to eat in Oak Bluffs. Kelli waited, impressed with how cheery Sandra was, despite the stress.

A Vineyard Love

"Sandra," Kelli said, as soon as the twenty-something left. "We have a big problem."

Sandra tilted her head. "What's going on, Kelli?"

"The painting in the foyer has been taken, as has Chef Billiard's knife," Kelli explained under her breath. "I'm beginning to think that all of this is related to the jewelry thief."

Sandra wrinkled her nose. "I hate to say it, but I'm pretty sure Miss Jennings and that other woman were just making that up to get a free room."

"That's what I thought, too. But my prize painting in the foyer is gone. And I checked the CCTV footage, and it's just a loop of the recent hours."

Sandra's eyes widened.

"You haven't seen anyone touch the painting, have you?" Kelli demanded.

"I haven't," Sandra said quietly.

"I'm going to ask others," Kelli said. "I don't have much hope, though. It's been such a crazy day. Maybe someone was able to slip out with it undetected."

"But there was a cop here," Sandra reminded her. "Wouldn't that have scared a thief off?"

Kelli frowned, sensing Sandra was right. "Maybe they have another way in. A way that allows them to slip in and out undetected." After a long, ponderous pause, she jumped up and said, "I have an idea!"

"What is it?" Sandra cried, but Kelli was too quick to answer, waving at Xander, who, on the other side of the foyer, was in conversation with one of the bell hops. "Xander! I'll be back!"

Xander nodded as Kelli again whipped back through the crowd, pausing for a moment to say hello to her little brother, Andy, one of her best friends in the world.

"You look happy!" Andy said, smiling in a way that reminded Kelli of Andy when he'd been a kid, long before he'd gone to war.

"I don't know about that. But I think I'm on the verge of figuring something out," Kelli told him.

Andy frowned. "Do you need help?"

"No! No. Keep having fun. I'll catch you later. We can talk during the reception!" Kelli said, as though she was sure every single fire would be put out by then. She had to believe it.

Kelli returned to the kitchen, where the chaos had stalled. Charlotte was nowhere to be found, but she'd left the boxes strewn across the kitchen again, and several of the kitchen staff members were angry about it. Kelli hurried around the boxes to the side door, where a number of vendor trucks sat. One of them was particularly huge, as it had brought the majority of the fresh fish, fresh vegetables, and alcohol they'd needed for the wedding.

Kelli approached this larger truck, her shoulders back. She needed to prove her dominance. A vendor worker stood out behind the truck, smoking a cigarette as he scanned his phone.

"Hi there!" Kelli greeted him and stopped a few feet away. "How's it going?"

The vendor worker puffed his cigarette, looking bored.

"I'm the manager of this hotel," Kelli explained.

"And I'm the vendor charged to deliver for this Harris wedding," he said half-sarcastically because it was obvious who he was. He couldn't have been anyone else.

Kelli felt he was purposefully trying her patience. She used the very last of her strength to continue to smile at him, which felt like a waste of energy. "Have you been out here all day?"

"Just got here around eleven-thirty," the man told her.

"And you've unloaded everything?"

"Not everything," the man told her. "The wedding planner has run in and out frantically, ordering us to bring this and that in and take this and that out. It's all such a delicate affair."

"Yes. The wedding planner is my sister," Kelli told him. "She's brilliant, one of the best in the business. But she can be hard to be around on wedding days."

Kelli wanted to get on this guy's good side, but the vendor hardly smiled back.

"Listen," Kelli said, placing her hands on her hips. "There has been a bit of difficulty here at the hotel today."

"Oh no," the man said, mocking her.

Kelli bristled. "Since you've been out here all day, I was curious if you'd seen anything. Anything fishy."

"I don't know what you mean, ma'am."

"Have you seen anyone take anything out the back door that they shouldn't have?"

"Why would I know what's supposed to come out?" the man demanded.

Kelli set her jaw. The man had a point, unfortunately, which meant she had to be straight with him. "I have a hunch that someone stole a painting from the foyer. It's worth a great deal of money."

The vendor opened his eyes wider, pretending he cared. This time, he didn't even bother to answer.

Kelli's arms fell to her sides. "Would you mind if I

look in your van?" she asked finally. "Just in case someone snuck out the painting and hid it..."

The man laughed at her. "We are under strict orders never to allow anyone who doesn't work for the business to enter the van. It all comes down to insurance. If you enter the van and something happens to you, we pay. And trust me, we can't afford to pay."

"I'll be so careful," Kelli said, sensing she was losing this game.

"Your version of careful could be our version of liable," the man told her. "Now, if you don't mind, lady, I'd really like to return to my work." As he stared at her, he removed another cigarette from the pack in his pocket and lit it.

Kelli glowered at him. "You need to be at least ten feet from the door when you smoke that."

Annoyed and smiling, the man took a large step back and continued to puff. Kelli peered behind him, through the darkness of the van, and tried to make out the strange shapes and boxes within. None of it looked like her stolen painting.

"If you see anything at all, will you contact me?" Kelli removed her business card and tried to pass it to him.

But the man laughed so that cigarette smoke puffed between them. "I don't take business cards, ma'am. I got a job."

Kelli then walked along the outer edge of the rest of the vendor vans, most of which were locked up, their drivers elsewhere. Frustrated, she continued to walk toward the edge of the cliff, where she had the instinct to scream across the frothing waters below. So many, many years ago, her grandmother had stood on this cliff and marveled at the strange and exhilarating new love she'd found with Robert Sheridan, a man who was not her husband. By contrast, Kelli's "stolen painting" situation seemed dumb.

Still, Kelli cared about the hotel. It had been a labor of love for her, a way to link her current family with the past. And she didn't want everything to fall apart.

Chapter Sixteen

It was an hour till the wedding. Amanda stood in only her slip, then laced her legs through the opening of her gown and allowed her mother and Christine to drape the top of the dress over her shoulders. With delicate fingers, Susan joined the pearl-shaped buttons in the back all the way up to her neck, then breathed a sigh. Amanda watched the transformation in the three-angled mirror in the bridal suite, where she became the bride of her dreams.

For a moment, every woman in the bridal suite was quiet, captivated with her. Amanda's eyes filled with tears, and Lola laughed and hurried forward with a Kleenex, which she helped place gently beneath Amanda's eyes to ensure the tears didn't mess up her makeup.

"I'm an idiot!" Amanda laughed, holding onto the Kleenex as her tears dripped into it. "It took almost an hour to get this makeup right."

"It only takes a second to ruin it," Lola said.

"I'm sure I'll ruin it by the end of the night," Amanda

said. "But I'd like to make it down the aisle first. And maybe take a picture or four hundred?"

Audrey sniffed and pressed her hands against her forehead.

"What's wrong?" Amanda asked.

"I'm trying not to cry, too," Audrey muttered. "But I can't stop thinking about how happy I am."

Amanda wrapped her arms around her cousin, her heart stirring.

"Amanda, I just love the colors you picked," Lola breathed, adjusting her periwinkle dress over her breasts and rotating so that she could see her back in the mirror.

"I figured it would suit all of your skin tones," Amanda said.

"It took her eight thousand years to decide," Audrey said mischievously. "Then again, I feel like every decision for this wedding was like that. Even your dress! Remember how many times we went back to the bridal shop?"

Amanda rolled her eyes at the memory. "I was such an anxious wreck."

"The woman at the bridal store no longer said hello to us when we came in," Audrey said. "She was so sure that Amanda wasn't going to buy anything. That she was wasting her time."

"Well, you proved her wrong," Christine said.

"Actually, I tried to return the dress the day after I bought it," Amanda remembered with a laugh.

"What!" Susan cried.

"I went with her," Audrey finished the story, "and begged her the entire way not to do it. I told her it was the perfect dress. But when we got to the store, the woman who worked there told us they'd recently instated a noreturns policy." Audrey cackled. "I have a feeling she made that up on the spot."

"It's funny. I felt so certain, at that moment, that I didn't want anything to do with this dress. But now, I can't imagine not having it," Amanda said, wrapping one of her glorious curls around her finger and sipping her champagne.

"Sometimes, the universe has to make up its mind for us," Audrey said. "It's just like how the universe brought us all back to the Vineyard for one reason or another. Me with my surprise pregnancy. Aunt Susan, with her divorce and her new and old love for Scott."

"Me, with my all-out obsession with that handsome sailor, Tommy," Lola said dreamily.

"And me, with my pastry business at the Bistro," Christine added.

"That and your love for Zach," Audrey reminded her.

Christine's cheeks burned red at the memory. Amanda watched as each of her aunts, her mother, and her cousin stirred with memories of the previous three years, enraptured by the choices they'd had to make to get to this moment.

Suddenly, there was a knock at the door. Amanda, Audrey, and Susan all called out, "Come in," in unison and laughed at themselves.

"We sound like a choir," Amanda said.

"Maybe we should start one. The Sheridan Women's Choir," Susan said.

The door opened, and Max's voice sailed through the crack. "Mama!"

"Max!" Audrey hurried to open the door wider, then

popped down to wrap her toddler in a hug. "How are you doing, buddy?"

Max was dressed in a little suit that Amanda and Audrey had hunted for at a little wedding boutique outside of Boston. His wild curls looked angelic and slightly sloppy, and his black shoes were very shiny and new.

"My shoes, Mama," Max groaned and pointed at them.

Audrey raised her head to smile up at the person who'd brought Max to see her. "Hi there, stranger."

Noah, her fiancé, stood in the doorway, waving nervously at Amanda, Susan, Aunt Lola, and Aunt Christine. Noah looked handsome, dressed to the nines to be Sam's groomsman, but his eyes stirred nervously, as though something was wrong.

"Is Max okay?" Audrey asked.

"What? Oh, yeah. Of course." Noah put on a grin that looked false. "I think he just hates his shoes."

"Do your shoes hurt, Max?" Audrey asked sweetly.

Max nodded so that his curls shook.

"Well, why don't we just take them off?" Audrey suggested, glancing over at Amanda. "I mean, they're not necessary, right?"

Amanda laughed. "I see no reason Max needs to wear shoes."

"Yeah!" Max raised his fists joyously as Audrey untied his shoes, then flipped them off. Now in only his socks, he raced around the suite, a free man, and said hello to everyone.

"He's such a ladies' man," Audrey said, rolling her eyes.

"Aud? Can I talk to you?" Noah asked, his tone difficult to decipher.

Amanda frowned and locked eyes with Audrey, who looked similarly worried.

"What is it? Is it about the wedding?" Audrey asked, wanting to keep things out in the open for Amanda's sake.

"No. Not really." Noah tried to laugh and palmed the back of his neck. "It'll only take a few minutes."

Audrey shrugged and followed Noah out into the hallway, leaving Max with the rest of them. Max was now at the window of the suite, his little hands gripping the ledge as he struggled to see over it. Christine walked over and lifted Max by the armpits so that he could see out.

"Look at that, Max! Do you see those cliffs?" Christine asked.

"Noah's acting weird," Susan muttered loud enough for Amanda to hear.

Amanda's stomach had already twisted into knots, which she was now trying her best to untie. "I'm sure it's fine," she told her mother and herself, her voice wavering.

Susan crossed her arms over her chest. "Audrey will tell us what's up when she comes back. And whatever it is, we can fix it." Susan's tone was difficult to read, but Amanda had a hunch she meant: *if Sam left you at the altar, we can figure this out.*

But, Amanda thought now, there wasn't really a way to "figure that out." Her knees felt like jelly, and she sat at the edge of the cream couch as Lola refilled her glass of champagne.

"We need more tunes," Lola said brightly, taking control of Audrey's phone to put on pop from the nineties, which was Lola's favorite era for music. As she danced, her eyes closed and her shoulders swaying, Amanda tried to smile.

Suddenly, Max was directly in front of her, smacking his hands together. "Auntie Amanda?"

"Hi, Max!"

"Why are you wearing such a big dress?" Max asked.

Everyone in the room was captivated by him, with the wonder on his face as he regarded Amanda in such a strange costume.

"Because I'm getting married today," Amanda explained. "And when women get married, they wear big, fancy dresses."

"Why?" Max asked.

Amanda laughed. "I wish I knew the answer to that. I guess we just want to look very beautiful on such a special day."

"Why?" Max asked again.

"Uh oh. Has he started the 'why' game again?" Audrey appeared back in the suite, her face ashen and her eyes very dark, as though she'd just learned something horrific.

"Mama!" Max cried again, rushing toward her. Audrey raised him against her and adjusted his legs around her waist. If Amanda wasn't mistaken, Audrey was avoiding her eyes.

"Audrey, what was that about?" Amanda asked, trying to keep her tone light.

"Oh. That was nothing."

"You look like you just learned something awful," Susan pointed out.

Audrey laughed, but it came out false. "Noah was just being Noah."

"Boys will be boys, right?" Lola tried to smooth the strange tension in the room.

"That's right," Audrey agreed with her mother.

Amanda literally couldn't get up. Her legs felt like lead. As Audrey re-opened the door to return Max to Noah, she murmured something too quiet for Amanda to hear. Then, she told Max, "Mama will see you later, baby. Okay? I love you so much!"

With the door safely closed behind her, Audrey skipped back to the group, refilled her flute with champagne, and smiled serenely at Amanda. "Gosh, I can't get over how pretty you look."

But Amanda didn't feel pretty just then. She felt like a mottled creature on the verge of experiencing yet another disastrous wedding. "Come on, Audrey. If it's really no big deal, why can't you tell me what Noah said?"

Audrey waved her hand. "I don't want to distract you today. Seriously. It's nothing. It's less than nothing."

"I know when you're lying, Audrey," Amanda told her. "It's just like when you ate the rest of the chocolate chip cookies after Max's birthday party and didn't want to tell me."

Audrey blushed crimson. "I did finally confess to that, though."

"Only because you had a huge stomach ache," Amanda said, finally finding a reason to laugh.

"Oh, gosh." Susan placed her hand on her chest and smiled, then hurried to take a photograph of the cousins. "Say cheese, girls!"

Amanda and Audrey cackled, threw their arms around each other, and grinned at the camera.

"My cheeks are going to hurt so badly by the end of tonight," Amanda said, deciding to focus on the positives rather than whatever Audrey and Noah were up to.

"That's the sign of a successful wedding," Christine said.

There was another knock at the door. Susan rushed for it, clearly on-edge, and opened it to find one of the downstairs hotel staff members, who'd brought the women a selection of pre-wedding snacks: slices of freshly baked baguette with various types of meats and cheeses, mini artisanal burgers, and mini cupcakes, slathered with cream cheese frosting.

"It'll be a long time till we're through the wedding and photography session," Susan explained as she placed the hors d'oeuvres out across the table in front of them. "Hours and hours until we can eat properly again. Besides. Amanda and I worked very hard to pick out the perfect hors d'oeuvres, and I think we deserve to enjoy them. Don't you think, Mandy?"

Amanda laughed, lifting a mini cheeseburger to her lips and eating delicately to ensure she messed up her makeup minimally.

"Lipstick can always be reapplied," Lola teased her. "You'll be doing plenty of kissing today, anyway."

"I kept mine in my bra during my wedding to Scott," Susan said mischievously.

"What a wonderful hack! Susan, I can't believe you haven't shared this before," Christine said.

Susan shrugged as she ate a piece of baguette, her eyes closing over the tantalizing morsel and the melted cheese. "All women have secrets."

Amanda, Audrey, Christine, and Lola howled with laughter, which eased the tension from Noah's surprise appearance. Slowly, as they filled their bellies, Amanda allowed her nerves to float out the window and out across the Aquinnah Cliffs. It was nearly showtime.

Chapter Seventeen

Xander's voice swept through the wind to find Kelli on the edge of the cliff. She turned as he approached her, his black hair whipping in the violent wind off the Sound, his smile big yet nervous. It occurred to her that she looked insane, standing at the edge of the cliff, as though she wanted to get as far away from the hotel as possible— even if that meant plunging into the depths below.

"There you are," Xander said, linking his fingers through hers. Warmth and assurance flooded Kelli, and she fell against him, shaking her head against his chest.

"I'm in over my head," she breathed.

"That's the understatement of the century," Xander said kindly.

"Did you ask the staff about the painting? Did anyone see who moved it? Or stole it?"

Xander sighed. "I talked to five different staff members, all of whom sped off after only a couple of seconds to tend to something else. Nobody seemed to know anything."

"Isn't that insane?" Kelli whispered. "I mean, it's a large painting."

"We'll track it down after this wedding," Xander assured her. "In the meantime, I really think we should take the next," here, he looked at his watch, "approximately fifty-five minutes to chat with your family, relax a little bit, and prepare to watch Amanda's wedding. We could get another round of Aperol Spritz and negroni?"

Kelli groaned. "You know what? That sounds like heaven on earth."

Kelli and Xander walked hand-in-hand back toward the front door of the Aquinnah Cliffside Overlook Hotel, where they entered directly in front of the empty space on the wall where the painting should have been. Kelli bit her tongue and forced her eyes away. Xander was right. She couldn't run around like a chicken with its head cut off to look for the painting, not with so many of her family members around. It was her duty to Susan, Amanda, and Charlotte to ensure this wedding went off without a hitch. The painting had nothing to do with that.

"There she is!" Steve, her older brother, appeared at the edge of the cocktail hour crowd, his grin sloppy and bigger than Kelli had seen it since the death of his wife, Laura. Beside him was his date, Rina, his daughter, Isabella, and her boyfriend, Rhett.

"Isabella, that dress is to die for," Kelli said, impressed with the young lady's dedication to vintage clothing.

"I got it at your boutique!" Isabella said.

"You mean Lexi's boutique," Kelli said. "She has total control these days."

Kelli's youngest, Lexi, appeared then, wearing a dark purple vintage dress she'd probably picked out for herself at the vintage shop, as well. Without hesitation, she wrapped Kelli in a hug and said, "This wedding is marvelous, Mom. I just love being in this hotel. It's like being in a fairy tale."

This was perhaps the sweetest thing Kelli had ever heard. "Are your siblings around here somewhere?"

Lexi waved her hand in the general direction of the fireplace, but Kelli couldn't find her other children in the sea of Martha's Vineyard faces.

"Will you be able to sit with us during the reception?" Lexi asked.

"I don't know," Kelli admitted at the same time Xander said, "Absolutely! We wouldn't miss it."

"Uh oh," Lexi said. "I don't know who to believe."

"Believe me," Xander said. "I've spent the better part of the past ten minutes convincing your mom to calm down a little bit and enjoy the fruits of her labor." Xander then waved at a passing waiter to order another negroni and Aperol Spritz. The waiter hopped to it, returning to Kelli and Xander with their drinks in fewer than five minutes. Kelli closed her eyes as she sipped her drink, swimming in sparkling water, bright orange Aperol, and champagne.

"I've never had that before," Isabella said.

"You must! It's Italian, just like you," Kelli said, remembering that Laura, Isabella's mother, had been part-Italian and had made the most delectable pasta recipes. In her own way, Kelli had mourned Laura since last September, sensing an enormous hole within the Montgomery family, one they would never fill.

Just as Kelli began to relax into the afternoon, however, she heard a sharp and alienating voice. It penetrated the crowd and quieted several members of her family, all of whom craned to hear.

A Vineyard Love

"I don't believe you understand what I'm telling you! They're gone. Do you speak English?" It was, yet again, Miss Jennings' voice, and it made Kelli's brain feel like it was on fire.

"I better go handle this," Kelli said, passing her drink off to Isabella. Before Xander could take her arm and remind her that she'd hired other members of staff for a reason, she burst through the crowd and wove her way back to the front desk, where Miss Jennings glowered at Henry, the poor guy handling the front desk. Henry looked at Miss Jennings as though she'd just threatened to eat him alive.

"Miss Jennings! Hello!" Kelli's voice was brighter than usual, perhaps due to the Aperol Spritz.

Miss Jennings glared at Kelli. "There you are. I've been looking for you all over the place. Were you... enjoying yourself?"

"What seems to be the problem, Miss Jennings?" There was always a problem with Miss Jennings. That was just her way.

Miss Jennings sniffed. "It's the strangest thing. You adjusted the safe. I watched you do it. And still, when I opened it not five minutes ago, I found that my bracelet and my necklace were both missing. Both, as I'm sure you can imagine, are worth much more than—"

"Than I make in a year," Kelli finished, wanting to mock her.

Miss Jennings flinched. "I need you to figure out where they went. It is preposterous that I entered this hotel last week and plan to leave tomorrow without any of my jewelry."

"I understand that," Kelli said. "Why don't we go up to your room together?"

The large clock in the foyer of the hotel said it was only forty minutes till the wedding. Kelli's heart threatened to burst with each beat. If she hurried with Miss Jennings, and perhaps if she left her with Officer Bobby again, she wouldn't have to miss the festivities. Not too much of them, anyway.

Miss Jennings and Kelli got into the elevator, which was immediately filled with the stench of Miss Jennings' very expensive perfume. Kelli's stomach tightened and stirred threateningly. Kelli imagined the Google review Miss Jennings would leave if Kelli got sick in the elevator. It wouldn't be pretty— but it did make her chuckle slightly.

"I don't believe you're laughing at my plight," Miss Jennings said.

"Absolutely not. I have something in my throat," Kelli explained.

When they reached Miss Jennings' room, Miss Jennings used her key card to open the door and guide Kelli through the first part of the suite. On the other side of the room, in the closet, the safe could be seen safely closed. As Miss Jennings glided toward it like a heavenly creature, Kelli paused near the vintage handmade desk, which she'd had Andy refurbish for this very suite.

What she saw on the desk gave her pause.

There, one directly next to the other, glinting in the light, were a bracelet and a necklace. Both were lined with diamonds and clearly very expensive— the sort of thing people in Kelli's world didn't travel with.

"As you can see," Miss Jennings was saying as she opened the safe, "they're gone."

"Aren't these what you're looking for?" Kelli pointed at the necklace and bracelet, too scared to touch them.

Miss Jennings peered across the room, her frown lines deep. "What? That can't be."

Kelli sighed and palmed her neck. Clearly, Miss Jennings was on a quest to make Kelli's life a living hell. Miss Jennings breezed through the suite and inspected the necklace and bracelet, then nodded. "How extraordinary," she said, as though they'd appeared from thin air.

Kelli wanted to remind Miss Jennings to look for her things before making accusations. She wanted to explain that she'd expected much more of her children when she'd been raising them. But instead, she smiled, feeling her brain nearly split in two from stress, and said, "Anything else, Miss Jennings?"

After Miss Jennings released her, Kelli stepped into the hall, closed the door, and placed her hands over her face. The world around her seemed to spin out of control, and her legs wavered beneath her.

Suddenly, the door burst open, and Miss Jennings was before her again. "Oh, good. You're still here. I wanted to give you a note about the breakfast. Of course, it was remarkably tasty, but..."

As Miss Jennings prattled on about breakfast, Kelli nodded along, her eyes flitting back and forth. Down at the opposite end of the hallway, something white burst past and then returned, and she furrowed her brow to see it properly. *Ah! Sandra.* She was probably hustling from one mess to another, just as Kelli was. Kelli had done a good job in hiring Sandra. At least she had someone good on her team.

But as Kelli stared down the hallway at Sandra, another figure appeared beside Sandra, speaking conspiratorially in Sandra's ear. Kelli's heartbeat sped up. She took a small step toward them as Miss Jennings continued to complain and realized with a horrific jump in her gut that the man Sandra was whispering to wasn't a stranger, nor was he a member of the hotel staff.

It was Sam.

Sam was all dressed up in his tuxedo, his bowtie as-yet untied and hanging down his chest. His face was red and blotchy, unlike how Kelli had ever seen it. Even during the height of chaos at the Sunrise Cove, Sam was always calm and composed. It was part of the reason people loved coming back to the inn— for the balm of knowing Sam.

Kelli's mouth tasted like cotton balls. *Why was Sandra speaking to Sam so closely, this far above the festivities down below? Wasn't Sam needed in his groom's suite? Where were the other groomsmen?*

During this chaotic moment, Kelli tried to make sense of it. Amanda and Sandra were, if not friends, at least friendly. Maybe Sam was asking Sandra about something, a gift he wanted to give Amanda. But if that was true, why wouldn't Sam just ask Audrey?

"Kelli? Are you paying any attention to me?" Miss Jennings blared.

Kelli forced her eyes away from Sam and Sandra, at a loss. Her stomach felt all wrong. "I hear you, loud and clear," she said. "And I will implement those changes."

Miss Jennings gaped at her. "What changes, exactly?"

Kelli was panicked. She tried to take a deep breath, but instead, she sputtered and said, "If you'll excuse me, Miss Jennings. I have to take care of something." She then turned on her heel and ran down the hallway, where, mysteriously, Sam and Sandra had disappeared. There was no sign of them at all. Kelli even opened the door to the stairwell and listened for the echo of footsteps, but there was nothing.

How could they have disappeared like that? Where could they have gone?

Kelli limped toward the grand staircase, praying that what she'd seen didn't matter, that it was a misunderstanding. *How could Sam cheat on Amanda?* It didn't seem likely. It didn't seem reasonable. Amanda was a gorgeous woman with big dreams and an even bigger heart. Despite her heartache after what Chris had done, she'd given Sam all of her love over the past two years. *Didn't Sam appreciate that?*

Chapter Eighteen

Thirty minutes before the wedding, Amanda received a text from her father.

> RICHARD: Hi, honey. I was wondering if I could see you briefly before the ceremony. My room is on the second floor.
>
> RICHARD: I know you must be very stressed and very busy, so don't worry if it doesn't work out.

Amanda showed the text to Audrey.

"It's cutting it close," Audrey said.

Amanda eyed herself in the mirror, noting her perfected lipstick, her sharp eyeliner, and her contours, which added dimension to her face.

"My only plan for the next thirty minutes was to freak out," Amanda said. "I might as well go see Dad to distract myself."

"Dad?" Susan said, turning from the mirror, where she'd been fixing her lipstick after the snack.

"He says he wants to see me," Amanda said as she walked slowly toward the door. Her mother's eyes glinted strangely, as though she wasn't willing to give Amanda up just yet. "I won't be long."

"We don't have very long until the ceremony," Susan said. "Charlotte just wrote she's sending people outside to begin taking their seats."

"It'll be fine," Audrey assured Susan. "We can't have the ceremony without the bride, anyway."

High on adrenaline, Amanda walked from the bridal suite toward the nearby elevator, where she stepped inside and pressed the button for floor two. She closed her eyes, inhaled sharply, then released, trying to shake off all the tension running through her. For some reason, she felt on the verge of a panic attack. When the doors opened onto floor two, she stepped out feeling weak in the knees and fell against the wall, her hand on her chest as she inhaled and exhaled.

"Amanda?" Her father's grounding voice found her ears, and a moment later, he was beside her, his hand on her shoulder. "Just breathe, honey. It's going to be okay."

Amanda raised her eyes to meet his and found herself floating on a cloud of memories of her long-ago girlhood. "Hi, Dad. Wow. You look good," she said, her voice very weak.

Richard dropped his hand from her shoulder and brushed it across his suit. "I look like an old man," he replied.

"Not true," Amanda said.

Richard nodded toward a group of cushioned chairs that overlooked the grand staircase and the ballroom. "Do you want to take a seat for a sec? I know you're needed for the big event soon. Thanks for letting me steal some Amanda time."

"Mom's freaking out," Amanda joked.

"I imagine she is. That's Susan Sheridan for you." He sounded sad about it, and not for the first time, Amanda wondered how much Richard regretted the divorce. At one time, Richard and Susan had been thick as thieves— and he just didn't have that same history with Penelope, even if he did really love her.

As Amanda assembled herself on the cushioned chair, her father on the one opposite, he smiled sincerely and said, "That dress is really something. You look stunning, honey."

Amanda blushed. "I feel a little bit silly. All eyes will be on me all day long. It's funny. I normally don't like all that attention."

"You deserve the attention today," Richard told her as he leafed through his breast pocket to remove a small jewelry box, which he passed to Amanda, sheepish.

"What is this?" Amanda asked, slowly removing the top to find an ornate locket in the shape of a heart. It looked vintage, perhaps from fifty to one hundred years ago. She drew it from the soft interior and held it aloft, peering curiously at her father.

"Open it," Richard beamed.

Amanda nodded and unclipped the opening so that the hinge swung open. Within the locket were two photographs, one on either side of the heart. The one on the left could have been Amanda Harris herself, as the smile, the hair, and even the expression were the exact same. Only the coloring of the photograph told a different story.

"It's Mom," Amanda breathed, captivated by the

image of her mother so many years ago— perhaps at Amanda's age.

On the right side of the locket was a photograph of Richard as a young man, as well. He was handsome and intelligent looking, the man who'd easily swept Susan Sheridan off her feet. The faces of the photographs were angled so that they seemed to be looking at one another across the locket. Amanda's head spun with confusion.

"I've never seen this before," she said.

Richard nodded. "I think your mother and I both forgot about it. I found it behind one of the armoires when I moved it to repaint the bedroom wall." He swallowed again, then added, "Penelope wasn't exactly pleased to have it in the house."

Amanda's heart thumped violently. *What did it mean that her father wanted to give her this?* But before she could muster the strength to speak, she heard a burst of footsteps down the hallway. The sound was almost violent and much louder than anything else in the hotel. Amanda popped up, her hand closed around the locket, and peered down the hall to see none other than Sandra! Sandra had stepped out of the elevator or the stairwell and was now running full blast down the hallway. Suddenly, she reached Room 222, stabbed her key through the knob, and tore through the door, out of sight.

"Huh," Amanda said with a shrug, her thoughts racing. Sandra had looked disheveled, her hair out of its normal bun and her uniform wrinkled. It didn't seem normal to Amanda that Sandra would be able to go in and out of guestrooms, either, especially when she was pretty sure that the hotel was fully-booked that weekend. *Did Sandra know someone staying at the hotel? Was her boyfriend staying there? Was that the reason for the wrin-*

kled clothing? Then again, given the chaos at the hotel, Sandra probably didn't have time to whip in and out of a lover's room.

What was it Sandra had said about her boyfriend? The last thing Amanda remembered was Sandra saying just how smitten she was with him. Amanda had felt, at the time, that Sandra had spoken about him as though they were teenagers— but in a naive way, not in a romantic way.

"What was that?" Richard asked.

"This friend of mine works here," Amanda said as she sat back down, returning her attention to the locket. "From what I can tell from her and Kelli's panic levels, this weekend has been very difficult for them."

"First week of the hotel jitters," Richard said.

"I hope they get the kinks worked out soon."

Richard was quiet, his eyes still on the locket. He obviously wanted Amanda to say something— something that told him how important the locket still was, even so many years after they'd filled it with photographs. Even so many years after Susan and Richard had signed the divorce papers and decided to get on with their lives without one another.

Amanda's eyes filled with tears, which she quickly blinked away. She hadn't thought to bring Kleenex with her.

"I'm sorry. I don't know what to say," Amanda breathed because it was true. The sight of these photographs, during a time when her parents had been in love, had stirred her soul.

"I just wanted to tell you that..." Richard stalled, peering out across the grand staircase. "I still remember how powerful that love was. And that it was the greatest gift of my life because it gave me you and Jake. Nothing will take away my memory of that time."

Amanda nodded, thinking she understood. Her father needed her to carry on this legacy, to know that his love for Susan Sheridan had been something special, something he shouldn't have thrown away so carelessly.

"Life goes on," Richard said simply. "And I'm just so glad that your life with Sam will start here, with me in the crowd."

Amanda leaned forward. "Dad? Can I ask you something?"

Richard nodded.

"Are you happy now? After everything that happened?"

Richard dropped her gaze, as though he wasn't sure what he wanted to reveal. "I'm happy, honey," he told her finally. "I'm really happy. I've found a new purpose. I'm a new and exhausted father. And life goes on."

Amanda wasn't sure what to make of any of this. But she stood with her father, wrapped her arms around him, and placed her cheek on his chest, listening to the beat of his heart. It was remarkable to grow up and learn that your parents had made buckets of mistakes. As a kid, Amanda had thought her father and mother had been Superman and Superwoman. It had seemed so clear.

"I love you, Dad. And I'm so happy you can be here for my wedding day," Amanda whispered. "I hope I'll see you out on the ballroom floor for the father of the bride dance?"

Richard's eyes widened with surprise. Amanda hadn't told him she was planning to uphold that tradition.

"There's nowhere else in the world I'd rather be," Richard said.

Chapter Nineteen

This couldn't be happening. Not again.

Kelli ran up and down the back staircase with her heart in her throat, thinking again and again of Sam and Sandra, of how close they'd been in the hallway, whispering as though they had enough things to tell one another to last a lifetime. She had no idea what to do with herself. Meanwhile, a glance out the side window showed that Amanda's wedding guests had begun to float out along the lush green grounds, still holding cocktails, as the string quintet set up and began to tune their instruments. It was nearly showtime.

Kelli reached the second floor, then rushed down the hallway to check on the bride and her bridal party. Just as she reached the doorway, Amanda appeared with a locket in her hand. She looked stricken, and her eye makeup was slightly smudged.

"Amanda! Are you okay?" Kelli cried, imagining that Sam had just found her and told her he was leaving.

Amanda's hand closed around the locket as she tried

to drum up a smile. "Oh, yes. I'm just silly. I messed up my makeup a little bit."

"What was that?" Susan Sheridan appeared in the doorway, grimacing. "Oh, Amanda. Get in here! Quick! We can fix it."

Amanda hurried into the bridal suite, into the welcome embrace of her mother. Susan locked eyes with Kelli just before she turned around and asked, "Everything good downstairs?"

"Looks like we're almost ready for you," Kelli said, puffing out her chest.

"This makeup job shouldn't take too long," Susan said. "As long as the bride doesn't cry anymore, we should be good!"

"Good luck with that," Audrey joked.

Kelli teetered on her heels and adjusted her hair behind her ears. "I'm going to find Xander and grab seats," she lied. "See you on the other side, Amanda! Love you so much."

Without waiting for a response, Kelli turned on a heel and rushed for the grand staircase, which she took toward the groom's suite. When she reached it, she took a deep breath, then pounded the door. A split-second later, Audrey's fiancé, Noah, opened it.

"Kelli! Hi!" Noah flashed her a confused smile. Behind him, Kelli could make out the rest of the groom's party— Sam's brother, Amanda's brother, and a few of Sam's friends from childhood. They sat on cream couches with beers, their bow ties tied, and their tuxedos glossy.

"Hey there. Just wanted to check up on everything," Kelli said. "The hotel has been chaotic today. I'm losing people and things like water through my fingers." She tried to laugh.

Noah palmed his neck and took a step back.

"I mean, where is Sam?" Kelli asked, trying to keep her voice light and bouncy, as though this was all a joke.

"Sam stepped out about fifteen minutes ago," Noah said, his voice darkening.

"Where did he go?" Kelli demanded.

"We're not totally sure," Sam's brother said.

Kelli's eyes opened wider. "You know that the wedding ceremony is in like fifteen minutes?"

The groomsmen gave one another nervous glances. Noah's face turned green.

"Can you call him? Text him?" Kelli asked, placing her hands on her hips.

Everyone was silent, which made Kelli's anxiety double.

"Wait," Noah said suddenly. "You said you're also losing things through your fingers? Not just people?"

Kelli shrugged. "I mean, guests keep reporting jewelry as stolen. And a beautiful painting in the foyer is gone. I don't know if it was moved for cleaning purposes or if there's something more sinister going on."

Noah gaped at her.

"Noah? What is going on? Stop looking at me like I have four heads!"

Noah stuttered. "It's just that, well. I didn't want to tell the guys yet..." Noah sighed and glanced back at the other groomsmen. "But I haven't been able to find the rings in over an hour."

Kelli's shoulders fell forward.

"Noah, are you serious right now?" Sam's childhood friend sputtered.

Noah dropped his gaze to the ground. "I told Audrey a little while ago, and she told me to keep looking. But I've

A Vineyard Love

searched everywhere. I even drove home, thinking I'd left them there. Nothing." He then flinched to add, "I don't know. Maybe they're wherever all the other jewelry is?"

Kelli gaped at him, her head swimming. *How was it possible that she'd come here to put out one fire only to learn about several new ones?* As the groomsmen gaped at Noah, mostly perplexed, Kelli muttered, "Noah? Can I talk to you in the hallway?"

Noah followed Kelli into the hallway as though he was a student getting in trouble at school and Kelli was his teacher. He hung his head. Kelli closed the door between them and the other groomsmen, "I'm going to ask you a question."

Noah looked stricken. "I really didn't mean to lose them, Kelli. I swear. I don't mean to toot my own horn, but I'm usually pretty dang responsible. I mean, I'm practically a father to Max, and..."

"It's not about the rings," Kelli cut him off. "It's about Sam."

"What about him?"

Kelli swallowed the lump in her throat. "Is it possible that Sam is having an affair?"

Noah's jaw dropped. "What?"

Kelli continued to stare at him icily.

"I mean, no? That's the most laughable thing I've ever heard?" Noah said, although he wasn't laughing. "What makes you say that?"

"I think I might have seen something," Kelli said.

"It's impossible," Noah said. "Honestly, that guy is crazy for Amanda."

But Kelli wasn't sure she could believe Noah. First off, she was pretty sure all men stood up for one another, no matter if they believed in one another's actions or not.

Secondly, maybe Sam was a mastermind, the sort of guy who'd been able to manipulate those around him easily. That handsome smile had taken him far.

It wouldn't have been the first time someone in the Sheridan family had been manipulated and taken for all they were worth. The Sheridans and Montgomerys believed in the goodness of people. They believed in second chances. Sometimes, that meant they got burned.

Kelli knew that firsthand. She'd been married to Mike for years— and genuinely had thought theirs was a true, fiery love, even when it had gotten emotionally volatile.

"If you're really sure," Kelli said, giving Noah another chance. "Because if you're marrying Audrey, Amanda has to come first for you. Not Sam."

Noah set his jaw. "I love Sam like a brother. I know he would never do something like this. Period."

Suddenly, from down below in the foyer, Kelli heard a strange and erratic voice. "Are you listening? It's all gone! It's all taken! Do you know how much it was worth?"

Something cold and hard fell into Kelli's stomach. Slowly, she tip-toed toward the edge of the staircase to peer down at yet another rich-looking woman dressed to the nines, screaming at a bell hop that her things were missing.

"Keep looking for the rings, and keep trying to get a hold of Sam," Kelli instructed Noah quietly. "We have fifteen minutes to make this wedding happen. We can't let Amanda down."

Chapter Twenty

Amanda stood in front of the double-wide glass doors downstairs, peering out at the two-hundred-plus guests who'd traveled from all ends of the United States to see her marry the love of her life. After nearly two hours of conversation and cocktails, they'd begun to quiet, sitting in white-painted chairs and glancing back toward the exit of the hotel expectantly, eager to see the bride. The string quintet continued to play "Pachelbel's Canon," perhaps for the third time, awaiting a cue from Charlotte that the bride was ready. Amanda had been scheduled to walk down the aisle two minutes ago, in fact.

But Noah had just stormed through the glass doors to announce that both the rings and Sam were missing. And Amanda couldn't very well walk down the aisle to nobody.

Behind Amanda, her mother, Aunt Christine, and Aunt Lola were dressed to the nines and whispering nervously, exchanging ideas on where to look for Sam. Amanda's friends from Newark were very quiet, giving one another glances that pitied Amanda. Only Audrey stepped forward and stood next to Amanda, her chin quivering with fear.

"I'm sure he's around here somewhere," Audrey muttered. "I mean, it's Sam. He loves you."

It felt as though a sword had sliced through Amanda's heart. She gave Audrey a look that meant, "come on," and Audrey pressed her lips into a thin line.

"I'm going through every single memory in my head," Amanda said. "From the moment we met each other to every single lunch, dinner, breakfast, sailing trip, road trip, and movie night we spent together. I'm thinking about this morning at three o'clock, when I saw his car lights beam through the night, and I genuinely thought, 'Wow. I finally found someone who loves me for who I am.'"

Audrey remained quiet, her eyes glinting with tears.

"I mean, am I the biggest fool in the world?" Amanda sputtered, closing her eyes.

"No! You're not." Audrey wrapped her hand around Amanda's wrist, as though she was afraid Amanda would float into outer space.

Amanda cleared her throat. "So, the reason Noah came to find you earlier was…"

"Because he'd lost the rings, yeah," Audrey said. "But I didn't want to tell you."

"Because you thought I'd fly off the handle," Amanda finished.

"I honestly figured Noah would find them by now. He's not normally so forgetful," Audrey explained.

Noah, who'd disappeared from the ballroom, returned, his face stricken because he'd just delivered the news that Sam was missing. Amanda thought that, next to her, he seemed the most likely to faint. Poor little guy.

"Have you seen Kelli, Noah?" Susan demanded, her voice strained.

Noah sputtered, and his gaze twitched right, then left. "She came to the groom's suite about twenty minutes ago. She was looking for Sam."

Amanda's eyes widened. "She already knew Sam was missing? Before anyone else?"

"I mean, I don't know. She seemed frantic," Noah said.

Amanda bit her lower lip.

"Did Sam know the rings were missing?" Audrey asked.

Noah nodded. "After I'd been looking for over an hour, I finally broke down and told him. Because he's the most patient guy in the world, he didn't seem angry."

"Maybe he ran off to look for the rings!" Audrey suggested, her face brightening.

"But that was ages ago," Lola pointed out. "And this hotel is big, but it's not that big."

"We would have seen him by now," Susan breathed.

Amanda's stomach twisted into knots. It seemed there were thousands of pieces to this puzzle, yet none of them were coming together to create a full picture.

Suddenly, from up on the second-floor landing came the sound of Kelli's stricken voice. Amanda raised her head so that she could just make out the top of Kelli's head, alongside two police officers' hats.

"My gosh," Susan breathed. "What's going on now?"

Another woman's voice sailed over the landing, accusatory and sharp. "It seems to me that you don't know the first thing about managing a hotel."

To this, one of the officers said, firmly, "This is no time for insults. Ms. Montgomery has just explained to you the procedure moving forward. We will do everything in our power to find your belongings, Ms. Penelope."

"I don't suppose you've ever had a two-hundred-thousand-dollar necklace stolen, Officer?" the woman demanded. "I don't suppose you've ever even seen a two-hundred-thousand-dollar necklace!"

"I haven't, no," the officer said. "But I imagine the insurance on something like that is pretty stellar." It was clear he was making fun of her, which probably would only make matters worse.

"Why don't you head downstairs and have a drink, Ms. Penelope?" Kelli tried to smooth things over. "Due to the wedding in the ballroom, our lounge is open, and we can offer you food and drink vouchers to get you through this terrible time."

"Drink vouchers?" Ms. Penelope said the words as though they were poison in her mouth.

"Gosh. Remind me never to be a hotel manager," Audrey muttered.

As Ms. Penelope turned to storm away and the police officers stepped together to speak quietly, Kelli walked to the edge of the landing, propped her arms up on the railing, and placed her face in her hands. Although Amanda was pretty sure she, the bride, was having the worst day of anyone, she thought Kelli might be in a close second.

Suddenly, Amanda bolted for the grand staircase.

"Amanda!" Audrey cried. "Where are you going?" Already, she was hot on her heels, with Noah coming up behind her.

Amanda had never flown up stairs in heels this

quickly before. Mercifully, she didn't break her ankle. When she reached the second floor, she gasped and straightened her back as sweat beads bubbled along the back of her neck.

Kelli turned and gazed at Amanda. She looked like the last-picked dog at the animal shelter.

"Oh gosh," Kelli said, her voice wavering. "You still didn't find him. Did you?"

Amanda's chest felt tight. She approached Kelli gently, aware that she was on the verge of bursting into tears. She felt as though she was at the very end of a terrible, heartbreaking movie— like in *Titanic* when Rose had to leave the dock without her love.

"Are you all right?" Amanda asked Kelli.

Kelli raised her chin. "I should be asking you the same thing."

Amanda leaned against the railing, peering out across the grand ballroom with its glittering chandelier and its mahogany bar.

"It's not hard to imagine this place one hundred years ago," Amanda heard herself say, her voice dreamy.

"That was my vision," Kelli said, her voice thin. "I'm glad you see it, too."

"It's like being taken back in time," Amanda said.

Kelli nodded and wiped a tear from her cheek. Through the big window, Amanda could just make out several of her wedding guests standing up from their white chairs with confusion and glaring at the double-wide doors. *Where was their bride? Hadn't they come all this way to see her? Didn't they deserve a show?*

"Why were you looking for Sam earlier?" Amanda asked finally, dreading the answer.

Kelli was quiet for a moment as she glanced back at

Noah, who shook his head. It was clear there was something Amanda didn't know.

"Just tell me," Amanda said. "Trust me. I've been through this before. It's better to rip off the band-aide."

Her voice had begun to sound more solid, as though she'd already begun to face her fate. She imagined herself two years from now, telling the story about how she'd been left at the altar twice. *"What luck I have!"* Maybe she would even find a way to laugh about it.

"I saw something," Kelli said finally. "Noah doesn't believe me."

"It's not that I don't believe you. I just think you saw something you didn't understand," Noah blared from behind them.

Kelli glowered at him, and the two of them had a face-off. The air was taut.

"What did you see, Kelli?" Amanda asked.

Kelli sighed. "I saw Sam really far down the hallway. He was with someone, whispering very secretively. It looked strange to me."

Noah rolled his eyes. "Sam wouldn't do this."

"Who was he whispering with?" Amanda demanded. "Just tell me, Kelli. I can handle it."

Kelli finally locked eyes with Amanda as her chin wiggled with sorrow. "It was your friend. My employee. Sandra."

And suddenly, all the color drained from Kelli's cheeks, her knees gave out from under her, and she collapsed across the carpet, abandoning the world.

Chapter Twenty-One

Chaos ensued after that. Amanda dropped to the ground to place Kelli's head on her lap and, in the process, tore the bottom of her dress. Little beads burst from the fabric and scattered across the floor like glitter. Meanwhile, Audrey hovered over the side of the railing and called her mother's name, saying, "Mom! Kelli passed out!" Noah raced to the nearest bathroom to pour her a glass of water, and Amanda curled Kelli's sweaty hair behind her ears and whispered, "Come on, Kelli. Come on. It's okay."

As time seemed to speed up around her, Amanda's head spun with what Kelli had just shared with her. *Sam and Sandra? Was it possible? How could it be?*

Amanda could remember only introducing Sam and Sandra once. It had been after yoga class a couple of weeks back, seven-thirty a.m. Sam had picked Amanda up for one reason or another, maybe to take her to breakfast, and Sandra had gushed about meeting him. *"I've heard so much about you! Amanda is over the moon with love for you. It sometimes makes a girl jealous."* Amanda had laughed it off. *But had there been something in the air between them? A sizzle?* Amanda now remembered that Sandra had spoken about her own love, a boyfriend she'd been "separated from" for a while. An art dealer.

Amanda's head thudded with a shattering headache. *Was it possible that this boyfriend Sandra had been separated from for a while was Sam? Had Sandra come to the island to get her ex back?* Amanda didn't know everything about Sam's ex-girlfriends, and she certainly didn't know their names.

Had Sandra befriended Amanda to get closer to Sam? Amanda closed her eyes as her thoughts raced.

"Hey! Amanda! We don't want you to pass out, too." Audrey nudged her, and Amanda opened her eyes to accept a glass of water. On her lap, Kelli had begun to open her eyes again, but her face was groggy and bloated, as though she'd just suffered an allergy attack.

Suddenly, Susan crouched beside Amanda and placed her hand on Amanda's shoulder.

"Hi, Mom," Amanda said, trying to make her voice light. "This is some wedding, isn't it?"

Susan couldn't smile. "I've just gone out to the grounds to announce that we need a little more time. The bartenders are stirring up more cocktails, and the speaker system is playing your wedding playlist. It gives us more time to look for Sam."

Amanda nodded. "Okay. Thanks." She felt dead inside.

"What happened?" Kelli moaned as she slowly shifted off Amanda's lap, rubbing her eyes and smearing mascara on her cheeks. She looked like a raccoon.

"You fainted, honey," Lola said. "When was the last time you ate?"

Kelli laughed ruefully. "Good question." She took another sip of water and crossed her legs beneath her. "Another guest was robbed. I can't make sense of any of it."

Lola and Christine exchanged worried glances. Nobody knew what to say— except for Audrey, of course, who blurted with, "Kelli? Did you really see Sam with Sandra?"

Susan, Lola, and Christine gaped with shock.

"Who is this Sandra girl? Where can I find her?" Lola demanded, ready to fight.

Kelli took another sip of water and nodded her head. "It breaks my heart to tell you," she said, although she couldn't look Amanda in the eye.

"Have you seen Sandra lately?" Susan demanded. "I mean, maybe she's with Sam somewhere?"

"Maybe they ran off together," Kelli said. "It would make sense. It's felt like I'm the only one keeping the hotel afloat for the past few hours."

"Wait," Amanda heard herself blurt. "I saw Sandra not that long ago!"

Everyone stared at Amanda as though she'd lost her mind.

"When Dad wanted to meet me," Amanda continued. "We sat on the second floor, right over there." She pointed to the cushioned chairs that overlooked the ballroom. "And I saw Sandra running frantically down the hallway. She looked super stressed, and I remember thinking that she was in over her head at the hotel."

"Where did she go?" Kelli asked.

Amanda pondered for a moment, thinking back only forty-some minutes ago when her life had felt very different. "She went into a room," she breathed. "I think it was 222."

Kelli's jaw dropped. "She went into a room?"

Amanda nodded.

"I'm sorry. It's just that we're completely booked, and there's no reason she should be going in and out of people's rooms. The maids are allowed to do that, but not this late in the day. We're very strict about that schedule," Kelli explained.

For a long moment, nobody knew what to say. Slowly, Amanda pulled herself up from the ground, gazing down at the beads that had popped from her dress. She no longer felt like the blushing, beautiful bride. She felt sharp and angry and ready to face whatever horrors awaited her. She didn't want to take this one lying down.

"Maybe Sam's in there, hiding out," Amanda suggested.

"I still don't think he would do that," Noah blared.

"Shut up, Noah!" Audrey cried. Lowering her voice, she added, "We can check for you, Amanda. But you shouldn't have to."

"I don't know that we can just go into a guest's room like that," Kelli said nervously. "I'm already off to such a horrible start at this hotel. If we storm into a guest's room while they're in there, I don't know if the hotel will recover."

Susan set her jaw. "Amanda? Are you sure it was Room 222?"

Amanda could see the room number planted in her memory, the 222 black and sure. Then again, the stress of the past hour had probably altered her brain chemistry. Nothing was for sure.

"Kelli, give me your master key!" Audrey said, her

face pale. "If Amanda's wrong, if someone else is in there, then you can tell the guests that I stole the key from you. I don't even care at this point. I just want to find Sam. I want to give him a piece of my mind."

Amanda had never seen Audrey so volatile. She looked like a warrior, ready to charge across land and sea to prove her love for Amanda. Kelli frowned, yet pulled the master key from her front breast pocket and passed it to Audrey, understanding that Audrey wouldn't stop demanding control until she got it. Audrey flipped the master key around and nodded at the rest of them.

"It's showtime," she said.

Chapter Twenty Two

Amanda and Audrey stood in front of Room 222, holding hands, as though they were about to leap from a great cliff and into the sea below. Audrey locked eyes with Amanda and muttered, "Are you ready for this?"

Amanda could hardly breathe. "Ready as I'll ever be."

Far down the hallway, Kelli, Aunt Lola, Aunt Christine, and Susan stood nervously, their arms crossed tightly over their chests. They watched Amanda and Audrey's reckless decision play out. Nobody knew what was going to happen next. Nobody knew what was on the other side of this door.

"Remember, if this doesn't turn out well," Audrey began, "I can tell Noah not to move in. We can just go back to the way things were. Heck, I'll even break up with Noah so we can spend more time together."

Amanda couldn't help but laugh. "What? Break up with Noah? Why would you do that?"

Audrey made a face. "You come first, Amanda. You know that."

And then, with a dramatic flourish, Audrey drew the master key into the doorknob and clicked the door open. She then shoved herself hard against the ornate door, stepped in, and beckoned for Amanda to follow her into the suite.

The suite was one of the more expensive ones, with two bedrooms, a living room with vintage furnishings and old, golden lamps and stylish mirrors. The door opened into the living room, which was dark, save for a television screen that played the news. The door clicked closed behind Amanda and Audrey, and they exchanged glances in the darkness. Amanda itched to turn on the light, but something in her told her not to. Her fears doubled, then tripled, and sweat pooled along her back. She had to remind herself, over and over again, that her mother was just outside. She would keep her safe.

Suddenly, from one of the bedrooms came a muffled scream. Amanda leaped forward, terrified, as Audrey ran behind her. As the muffled scream continued, it felt like they were going in slow motion, as though they would never reach the door to the bedroom.

When they did, Amanda snapped on the light to reveal a horrific sight.

There, on the king-sized bed, was Sam.

Sam was wearing his wedding tuxedo, his hair was gelled perfectly, and even his Italian-suede shoes were glinting in the light. But he'd been tied to the bed with what looked to be scarves wrapped tightly around his ankles and his wrists. In his mouth was another scarf, through which he'd screamed. His eyes were rimmed red and filled with tears.

It was the worst thing Amanda had ever seen.

"Oh my God!" Amanda flung forward, ripping her dress yet again, and removed the scarf from Sam's mouth.

Sam sputtered, inhaling as much oxygen as he could and nearly choking himself. "Amanda! How did you find me?" His face echoed relief.

Audrey attacked Sam's ankles, untying the scarves. "These knots are crazy. Did a sailor do them?"

"Baby, what happened to you?" Amanda whispered.

Sam shook his head violently. He looked out of his mind. "It's her. It's that horrible woman from your yoga class."

"Kelli said she saw you two together?" Amanda continued. "What were you doing?"

"I had a hunch she'd taken the rings!" Sam cried. "And I followed after her and cornered her. And then, suddenly, I lost consciousness. She must have drugged me?" His panic continued to mount.

"Shh," Amanda breathed. "We'll get you out of this."

"Is she armed?" Audrey rasped.

"I thought I saw a knife, but I can't be sure." Sam paused, then added, "I have no idea what these people are capable of."

"These people?" Audrey demanded. "Who else?"

"She's with some guy," Sam explained. "A muscular guy she seems to be in love with— who, I have to say, doesn't seem to be half as in love with her. Not that I'm an expert on criminal romances. Anyway, they keep coming in and out the back door to take stuff out." Sam nodded toward a door that Amanda had previously thought led to a closet.

Audrey hurried for the door and opened it to find a back staircase. "Where does it go?"

"It must drop out near the back of the kitchen," Sam said. "I think it's a fire escape."

"What have they been taking out of here?" Amanda asked.

"I don't know! Stuff. Fancy-looking stuff. Vintage furniture. Jewelry," Sam said. "My guess is they wanted to use the wedding as a distraction as they took whatever they wanted. When I caught her with the rings, I got myself involved in something a lot bigger than I thought." Sam trailed off, his eyes misty. "Amanda, I'm so sorry. You must have thought that I'd left you."

Amanda could hardly breathe. Her eyes heavy with tears, she fell forward and kissed Sam with her eyes closed, then whispered, "I love you so much, Sam. I was so frightened we wouldn't get to spend the rest of our lives together."

"I love you, too," Sam said tenderly, kicking his legs, which Audrey had removed from their ties. "We can't waste any time, though. I heard them talking. Sandra is scheduled to bring another load to their van downstairs in about ten minutes. Her boyfriend will be waiting down there, at which point she's supposed to leap into the van. This island's small, but it's not that small. They could easily hide out somewhere with that stuff, lay low, and get away with it." Sam frowned, heavy with contemplation. "Which means you need to call the cops immediately—and you also need to tie me back up."

Amanda's jaw dropped. "Absolutely not."

"That's insane, Sam," Audrey affirmed.

"Sandra won't hurt me if she doesn't think I know anything else," Sam said. "I can tell. She's weak, and she's terrified. She cried the entire time she tied me up. I'm pretty sure she just wants to do whatever her boyfriend tells her to do."

"Sam..." Amanda repeated his name as the pressure in her chest mounted.

"Amanda, she's coming back in less than ten minutes to take the rest of the stuff. If I'm not here, she'll freak out, and it's possible that her boyfriend will get away with all those stolen goods."

Amanda and Audrey locked eyes, having an entire, wordless conversation within the span of fifteen seconds.

"Have the cops at the back entrance to nab Sandra and her boyfriend," Sam said. "You should both go downstairs and pretend nothing's wrong."

"Are you crazy?" Amanda shot.

Sam gave her a look, one of love and compassion and impatience. "Come on, Amanda. It's the only way."

As gently as she could, Amanda slipped the scarf back between Sam's lips as Audrey quickly tied him back up. "I didn't get the knots right," Audrey said, "but I doubt Sandra will notice." Afterward, Amanda kissed Sam on the forehead and whispered, "I'll see you at the altar, baby," before she fled toward the doorway, raced down the hallway, and headed straight for Kelli.

"Kelli! We need to get downstairs," Amanda said, taking Kelli's elbow.

Kelli, Lola, Susan, and Christine sputtered with disbelief.

"What happened in there?" Susan demanded.

"It's hard to explain," Amanda said. "But Kelli. Are the cops still here? We need their help ASAP. Time is of the essence."

Kelli drew her phone from her back pocket and sighed. "I have them on speed dial at this point."

A Vineyard Love

As quickly as she could, Amanda explained what she knew: that Sandra would be making a final delivery of stolen goods from Room 222 within the next fifteen minutes and that it was essential the cops see it happen from the back door. That way, they could apprehend both Sandra and the boyfriend at the same time. Kelli looked mystified.

"So that's who took everything!" she cried. "And gosh, yes. It makes total sense why they'd book Room 222 for this. It's one of the only rooms with a fire escape out the back. Only people who work here know that."

As Kelli dialed the cops, Amanda and Audrey walked down the grand staircase, both petrified. When they reached the foyer and then entered the ballroom, they found that the entire wedding party had returned to the ballroom to order more cocktails. Their gossip was a dull roar, and their faces flashed with a mix of curiosity and pity.

Before Amanda could escape from all the turmoil regarding her future, Charlotte made a beeline for her. In all the chaos upstairs, Amanda had forgotten that the wedding player probably had had a full-on anxiety attack. She'd lost the bride, the groom, and the bridal party, all in a matter of a half-hour.

"Amanda!" Charlotte touched her arm gently and frowned. "Do you want to go back upstairs? Oh, and what happened to your dress?"

Amanda waved her hand. "I'm going to mingle for a while," she explained.

"Did you find Sam?" Charlotte demanded.

"Sam just needs a few more minutes," Amanda explained. "In the meantime, we should drink some cocktails, don't you think? I know you're my wedding planner, but I want you to enjoy today just as much as everyone else!"

Charlotte gaped at her, then turned on her heel to speak into the microphone that hung near her mouth. As she hurried away, she said, "I found the bride, Rachel. But there's something off. Keeping tabs on the situation."

Even though they pitied her, one of the staff members approached soon with glasses of white wine for both Amanda and Audrey. Several guests, most of them from Sam's party, glanced at Amanda and didn't say anything, so she downed one-half of her glass of wine and said to Audrey, "I feel like the belle of the ball."

Audrey cackled nervously and nodded toward the foyer, where the two officers who'd been at the hotel earlier stood in conversation with Kelli. Kelli explained everything with fluttering hands, and the cops quickly cut through the foyer and back through the kitchen, where, hopefully, they would snatch up Sandra and her man.

"Hi, honey!" Aunt Kerry appeared, wearing a strained smile. It seemed like she'd taken it upon herself to cheer up Amanda, the jilted bride. "The white wine here is divine. Did you pick it out?"

"Amanda left no stone unturned at this wedding," Audrey said.

"I know you're already a brilliant lawyer, but you should really look into party planning on the side," Aunt Kerry said, her voice overly polite. "You're so detail-oriented, and you have brilliant taste, just like your mother. Ah, there she is! Hello, Susan!"

Susan appeared beside Amanda, wearing a smile that echoed Amanda's nerves.

"I was just telling Amanda that she should really look into event planning," Aunt Kerry said. "You know, some women are meant to be career focused. And really, I mean, marriage and children can be distractions from what we really want in life."

Amanda wanted to laugh. Obviously, Aunt Kerry wanted to console Amanda, as she'd decided Amanda would never be married or have children of her own. *Who in their right mind would try to get married after two failed weddings?*

"I think Amanda will be just fine juggling marriage, motherhood, and her law career," Susan said proudly.

"I learned from the best," Amanda said as she placed her head on her mother's shoulder.

Meanwhile, Aunt Kerry gaped at them, blinking from mother to daughter, as though she was certain they'd lost their minds. Maybe they had.

Chapter Twenty-Three

Immediately after Amanda and Audrey had glided downstairs to mingle with wedding guests, hopefully indicating to Sandra that nothing was amiss and that nobody was the wiser, Xander had bolted from the stairwell and appeared on the landing to find Kelli, Susan, Lola, Christine, and Noah in shock. Just a few doors away, Sam apparently sat, bound, and gagged, awaiting Sandra's return. And none of them could be in that hallway when she made her appearance. It would foil Sam's plan.

After Kelli had quickly explained everything to Xander, during which time he'd stared at her, his jaw slack, she'd asked him to stand at the railing of the third floor, where he would have a view of the second-floor landing. "When you see Sandra whip down the hallway, text me immediately. Then, I can alert the cops that she's on her way downstairs."

With Xander now set up on the third floor, watching, and the police officers in plain clothes watching the back entrance, Kelli felt jittery and nervous and unsure what to

A Vineyard Love

do with herself. She stood at the edge of the wedding crowd, watching as Amanda blushed crimson with embarrassment as Kelli's mother, Kerry, tried to make her feel better about being jilted at the altar. Amanda was playing the part well, probably because she'd done it all before.

Gosh, Kelli was exhausted. That fainting episode had terrified her. Her head remained cloudy, but her motivations were clear. It wouldn't be long until this nightmare was over.

Still, she couldn't help but blame herself for promoting Sandra so quickly. She'd allowed herself to be manipulated by her, to be drawn into her kindness. Kelli now had a hunch that Sandra had framed Piper and forced Kelli to fire her, if only so that Sandra could get the master key to herself. Kelli made a mental note to hire Piper back immediately. Maybe she would even promote her.

Suddenly, Kelli's phone buzzed.

XANDER: Incoming.

Kelli's heartbeat escalated. As though she ran from a fire, she headed toward the kitchen with her heart in her throat, where Chef Billiard continued to berate his sous chef. "I can't believe nobody is willing to confess to stealing my knife! Do you know who I am?" It seemed his insults had no bounds, which also seemed expected amongst kitchen staff who respected their chef.

Kelli tucked herself in the shadows of the back hallway, separated from the kitchen by a single wall. From here, she could see the door that led to the fire exit stairwell, down which Sandra was bound to come soon. As her legs wavered dangerously beneath her, Kelli prayed she wouldn't faint again. She wanted to see this— and she also didn't want her weakness to indicate to Sandra that something was amiss downstairs.

Before Kelli could drown in any more anxious thoughts, a woman in sunglasses and a big black hoodie burst from the fire escape doorway. She had a massive black backpack over her back, probably filled with goods from the hotel and from hotel guests— all of which she'd deftly pocketed as the guests and Kelli had been elsewhere and discombobulated. Sandra even had the nerve to wave to one of the kitchen staffers and say, "Hope you guys are holding up okay? It's crazy out there! But that's just weddings, right?" The kitchen staffer laughed.

Sandra bolted from the exit after that into the shining light of a beautiful afternoon. Kelli tip-toed to the doorway to peer out as Sandra traipsed directly to the van in question. Kelli couldn't believe it: it was the same van she'd wanted to search a few hours before. The same "vendor" she'd spoken to walked from the darkness in the van, placed his hands on Sandra's cheeks, and then kissed her with his eyes closed.

At this moment, they felt like Bonnie and Clyde, as though nothing in the world could get them down, as though they were the two smartest people in the world.

"Stop! You are under arrest." Officer Bobby's voice echoed through the vendor vans and made Kelli's spine shiver with its power. "Separate, put your hands up, and walk slowly down the ramp of the van. No sudden movements."

Kelli fixated on Sandra's face as her kiss with her criminal lover broke. All the blood drained from her cheeks as she staggered away from her boyfriend, who glared at her and began to spit insults. "What the heck did you do wrong, Sandra? Huh?" He grabbed her shoulders and shook her like a rag doll.

"Hey! Stop that!" Kelli couldn't stop herself. She was too exhausted, swimming in memories of Mike's cruelty. "Let her go!"

"Put your hands UP!" Officer Bobby called, approaching from the left of the vendor van as the other officer approached from the right. Officer Bobby had drawn a gun, and his jaw was sharply clenched.

Sandra's boyfriend released Sandra's shoulders, which resulted in her falling off the ramp and onto the hot pavement. There, crumpled up on the ground, she raised her arms and began to sob.

"Give it a rest, Sandra," the boyfriend ridiculed her as the cops got closer. He then yanked himself around to peer through the shadows of the back of the van, as though weighing up the probability that he could leap through the mess of boxes and vintage goods and get to the driver's seat. Even from where Kelli stood, it looked very unlikely.

"I'm going to tell you one more time," Officer Bobby warned. "Put your hands up."

With a dramatic roll of his eyes, as though he was just a teenager who'd been caught staying out too late, the man raised his hands and shrugged his shoulders. Things sped up after that, as though Kelli was fast-forwarding through a criminal show on television. Officer Bobby walked toward the thief and managed to manipulate his body so that his torso fell forward and his wrists were cuffed together in one fell swoop. Kelli was impressed. Sandra was much easier to handle, of course, as she'd turned to putty in the officers' hands. Even still, they couldn't trust her, removing the backpack filled with hotel things before they cuffed her. As the other cop pulled her to her feet, Sandra turned spontaneously to meet Kelli's gaze. Sandra's jaw dropped. For a moment, they regarded one another— both bleary-eyed and exhausted for very different reasons. Kelli couldn't believe it. Her heart broke for this poor, stupid creature, so young and so naive, who'd obviously allowed herself to be manipulated by her criminal boyfriend.

Kelli had fallen for Sandra's tricks. Maybe it had hardened her for the future. Maybe she would move forward in time with the knowledge that very bad things could happen, even with the best intentions.

As the cops shoved Sandra and her boyfriend into the back of the cop car, Kelli walked toward the vendor van, which remained open like a mouth. On the ramp, she peered inside to find mountains of boxes and bags. Toward the back was something long and large and thin, wrapped in paper. With a nervous jump in her gut, she approached it and tore at the edges of the paper to peer inside. Just as she'd suspected, it was the painting that had been taken in the foyer. How had they managed that? It was incredible.

"Kelli?"

Kelli leaped out of her skin and turned around, gasping, to find Xander on the ramp. His face was drawn. Kelli staggered toward him, threw her arms around him, and shook violently. Although Kelli hadn't known he was capable, he slowly lifted her up and carried her down the ramp, away from the van, and back into the sunlight, where she sat on the lush grass for a quiet moment. The cop car's tires cracked over the gravel on the edge of the parking lot as they returned to Oak Bluffs. It had been one hell of a day.

"That was absolutely crazy, Kelli," Xander breathed, his hand on her cheek as he gazed into her eyes.

"At least I know I wasn't going insane, though. Things really were going missing. They were stealing things, right and left," Kelli said.

Xander nodded wordlessly.

"Hey! They're here!" Audrey's voice came from the doorway to the kitchen before she burst into the sunlight, still in her bridesmaid dress. Amanda and Sam hurried up behind her, bride and groom, hand-in-hand. Amanda and Sam looked world-weary and fearful, the same way they'd looked after their car accident last year. These poor kids, Kelli thought now. They'd already been through so much, and they hadn't even made it down the aisle yet.

"Are you okay?" Amanda said, perching gently beside Kelli. There were now two rips at the bottom of her wedding dress, and more beads had scattered off, leaving behind ghost-like strings.

"Oh, Amanda. I'm so sorry your wedding is ruined," Kelli breathed.

Amanda's face glowed with surprise. "It's not ruined, Aunt Kelli. Not in the slightest."

"Come on," Kelli said, gesturing vaguely toward the van.

Amanda placed her hand over Kelli's in the thick grass. "It has not been the easiest day of any of our lives," Amanda said. "But everyone I love is still here. Sam didn't take off the minute he saw the altar. And those criminals are long gone, now— they're the cops' problems and not ours." As she tried to smile, her face seemed to get the hang of it, and she began to beam like the bride she was.

"We can clear another day in the schedule," Kelli

tried, wanting to fix this. "Any day, all summer long. We can do this all over again."

But Amanda wouldn't hear of it. "I want to marry Sam today. That is, if Sam's still up for it."

Sam pressed his forehead against Amanda's, his breaths coming in fits and starts, as though he'd just run a marathon or held his breath for too long. When he locked eyes with Amanda, there on the lawn that encircled the tremendous and historical hotel, Kelli felt she could see everything that would come after this for them— the wedding, the babies, and the life-altering decisions that went hand-in-hand with middle age and even the shattering reality of death. Kelli blinked back tears, remembering that life was something none of us got out of alive. But somehow, during the small era of time that she and Amanda had been on this earth, they'd both been able to find their person. It was truly an incredible thing.

"I don't just want to marry you today, Amanda Harris. I need to," Sam told her, which settled it. Amanda gasped with relief.

Chapter Twenty-Four

The full breadth of the story wasn't reported to the wedding guests that afternoon. Kelli gave them an abbreviated and PG version, saying, "We've had a bit of a mix-up today, which means that the wedding is postponed to six-thirty. The bride needs a little more time to prepare, and the hotel manager needs a drink." The guests laughed nervously across the ballroom, shifting their weight and blinking hungrily at one another. It had been several drinks since they'd had the appetizers. From above, where Amanda watched them on the landing of the staircase, Amanda realized they needed to feed them as soon as possible, or they would have another disaster on their hands.

Amanda returned to the bridal suite, where Audrey was at the tail-end of explaining the dramatic story of what had happened to Brittany and Brooke, who'd been drinking with friends from Newark. Lola, Susan, and Christine were fixing their makeup and watching Max, who remained shoeless, bouncing around the room with manic eyes that told Amanda just how much he needed a nap.

"We need to feed everyone," Amanda said. "Maybe we should serve the reception dinner early?"

Susan raised her mascara wand thoughtfully. "I don't know, honey. Are you sure you want that? Won't that screw up the schedule of the wedding?"

Just as she finished saying it, Susan, Amanda, and Audrey burst into giggles.

"I'm sorry. I just realized what I said. Like the wedding schedule isn't screwed up already!" Susan laughed. "But then again, you can do whatever you want with today, Amanda. It's all yours. If you want to order sandwiches for everyone to tide them over, be my guest."

"Do you think anywhere in Oak Bluffs is willing to serve two hundred sandwiches out of the blue?" Amanda asked.

"You can spread out the orders," Audrey suggested. "There's got to be at least fifteen sandwich places across the island with the capacity to make between ten and fifteen sandwiches. We can tell them it's an island emergency." She gave Susan a knowing smile and added, "Susan Sheridan always knows how to get what she wants. Let's put her in charge."

Susan grabbed her phone and sped off. "I'm on it."

Amanda sat at the edge of the chair in which she'd been only a couple of hours before, getting the final touches on her makeup and hair before the ceremony. Now, in some respects, she looked a bit crumpled around the edges. Her lipstick had smeared, her eyeliner had drained down her cheeks, and her contours made her face look ghastly and strange. With a heavy sigh, she reached for a makeup cleanser and began to smear it off as, behind her, Audrey said, "I think it's time for round two!" and turned on the speaker system to play "...Hit Me Baby One More Time."

Amanda whirled around, cackling. "You've got to be kidding me."

"Just one more time, Amanda," Audrey said as she whirled around and sat on the chair beside her, leaning toward the mirror to look at her own mussed makeup. "It's only the third time you'll get ready for your wedding. And they say the third time's the charm, don't they?"

Just as she'd said she would, Susan saved the day yet again. In a half-hour's time, delivery drivers from sandwich and pizza restaurants across the entire island whizzed through the parking lot, popping from cars and vans with piles of food and pouring through the Aquinnah Cliffside with goofy smiles. From above, Amanda and Audrey watched as the wedding guests tore toward the drivers like wild dogs.

"This was a good idea. These hungry people could have ruined your wedding," Audrey joked.

Kelli, Charlotte, Rachel, and other hotel staff members hurried around, setting up little tables with piles of paper plates. Other staff members appeared to take more drink orders, their *yes, sirs* and *yes, ma'ams* echoing through the ballroom.

"Look! There's Sam and Noah!" Audrey pointed at their two loves, who stood in the midst of the crowd with big sandwiches, their smiles greasy.

Suddenly, mischievous, Amanda grabbed Audrey's hand and led her down the staircase. Her stomach thundered with hunger, the kind she couldn't quell with just a salad and a few sips of water. Sometimes, life called for sandwiches. Sometimes, life called for grease.

"What's gotten into you, Amanda Harris?" Audrey cried as they bounded toward the foyer, then turned to face the wedding guests.

"There's the bride!" Grandpa Wes called, waving from where he ate slices of pepperoni pizza with Beatrice.

The crowd quieted to peer at her curiously, each of them remembering just how fearful they'd been only an hour before when they'd thought she was getting dumped again. Now that they were well-fed, they could appreciate the messiness of the day. It was more cinematic than any wedding anyone had ever been to. The stories would last forever.

Amanda walked through the crowd, saying hello to everyone she met, blushing graciously as they told her how pretty she looked. Long before she'd assumed she would meet Sam, he appeared through the crowd to find her, and she threw her arms around him and hugged him as, around them, the crowd sighed with disbelief at the beauty of their love.

"I'm sorry," Amanda said. "I heard it's bad luck to see the bride before the wedding."

Sam cackled and gestured toward the pile of sandwiches on the table nearest them. "You want a chicken sandwich?"

"I don't think I've ever been hungrier in my life," Amanda said. "It feels like I've been dieting for this wedding forever at this point. I'm so over it."

"No more diets," Sam told her. "That's my number one rule for our marriage."

"Ha." Amanda crumpled against the table, unwrapped her sandwich, and dug her teeth into the crunch of the toasted bread and the decadent and savory

Greek flavors of the chicken sandwich, which had been slathered with tzatziki. "Oh my gosh," she moaned after she swallowed, closing her eyes.

Sam rubbed the top of her back and laughed. "Eat up, baby. We've got quite a day ahead of us."

Amanda cackled as Sam used his napkin to wipe her chin of lipstick, telling him, "Lipstick can always be fixed. Everything can always be fixed. As long as we're together."

Sam's eyes watered with tears as he fell forward and kissed her. Around them, the wedding guests roared, their applause mounting. They hadn't even been married yet, and Amanda already felt on top of the world.

Chapter Twenty Five

The string quintet, all of whom had feasted on pizza and sandwiches and drunk at least one cocktail during the afternoon break, set up outside in the evening sun at six to warm up. From upstairs in the bridal suite, Amanda heard the swells of their strings, drawing out across the grounds of the hotel and across the water along the cliffs. Her makeup perfected and her heart on her sleeve, she again descended the grand staircase with Audrey, Lola, Christine, Susan, Brooke, and Brittany, prepared to welcome the next era of her life as someone's bride.

At the double-wide doors downstairs, Charlotte nodded firmly, ready to take full control over the rest of the festivities. When "Pachelbel's Canon" started up again, she opened the doors to reveal the two hundred guests, all seated in white chairs, waiting.

Brooke and Brittany stepped out first with their chins lifted as they strode down the aisle between the white chairs and lined themselves up, watching as next came

Christine, then Lola, followed by Audrey, who, before she headed out, squeezed Amanda's elbow, and said, "I'll see you on the other side."

Now, it was just Susan and Amanda, mother and daughter, their hearts fluttering like hummingbirds in their chests as they listened to "Pachelbel's Canon" shift to the string version of a song Sam and Amanda adored: "At Last" by Etta James. The song was so linked to Amanda's heart that it immediately triggered tears, which she blinked back.

"You can let them fall, honey," Susan said, raising her elbow for Amanda to take. "Nobody's going to remember your makeup today. That's for sure."

Amanda laughed in a way that nearly descended into sobs and strung her arm through her mother's. "Thank you for getting me here, Mom. I wouldn't have had the strength to get better after last time without you."

Susan frowned. "You would have been fine without me. You're stronger than you think you are, Amanda. The entire family looks to you for strength, compassion, and help. And you give it so selflessly. As your mother, I've learned much more from you than you could even imagine."

Amanda was caught off-guard at this confession, as she'd never imagined her mother had learned anything from her. Not the great Susan Sheridan. Not one of the most successful defense attorneys on the east coast.

"Hey!" Charlotte hissed from the side of the foyer. "It's time to go!"

Arm-in-arm and completely in sync, Susan and Amanda stepped onto the grass, walking in time to "At Last" as the wedding guests stood to take them in. It was funny that they put their hands on their chests and craned their heads to see, as Amanda had spent the better part of the afternoon chummy with them in the ballroom, eating a chicken sandwich as though it was just another Tuesday. But out there on the rolling grounds of the historic hotel, as an early moon floated glassily in the dying blue sky, Amanda sensed what the rest of them did: there was magic here, at this wedding, and across the entire island.

As Amanda passed her brother and her father, she smiled at them extra hard, wanting to translate her love for them. Jake looked on the verge of bursting into tears, a rarity for him, as he'd never been very in touch with his emotions.

Sam waited for Amanda at the top of the aisle, dapper as ever in the tuxedo they'd selected together on a random afternoon in Boston when the idea of their wedding had been a distant star. Although he'd seen her for hours in her dress, his eyes glinted with tears. This was it.

As Susan passed Amanda off to Sam, she kissed her gently on the cheek and whispered in her ear, "Go get 'em, tiger." Amanda laughed so hard that a tear shook from her eye. "I love you," she whispered back.

Amanda stood before Sam, clutching her bouquet as though it could keep her stable, as Pastor Carter, the minister from the Newark church she'd been raised in, began to speak.

"Good evening, everyone. We are gathered here today in holy matrimony to celebrate the love between Amanda and Sam, two absolutely wonderful young people I've had the pleasure to get to know over the past few months, as they've spoken to me about their desires for this service,"

Pastor Carter said. "I must admit that in all my years of working weddings, this has to be the most dramatic of them."

The crowd laughed appreciatively as Sam reached out to take Amanda's hand.

"But as they say, love always finds a way, even through the most difficult of circumstances," Pastor Carter continued. He then side-eyed Noah to add, "I've also been told that, in all the kerfuffle earlier, the rings are not available for use. Apparently, they're now in police custody as 'evidence.'"

"Ohhh," the wedding guests hissed and cried out.

"But as you know, the wedding ring is only a symbol of Amanda and Sam's love, which means that today, something else can serve as that symbol until Amanda and Sam get the rings back," Pastor Carter explained as Noah hurried forward to hand off the "stand-in rings," which were, it looked like, mood rings, the kind that changed colors with your "mood," supposedly.

"Noah? Is this the best you could do?" Pastor Carter held them up as the crowd, Amanda, and Sam laughed. Noah just shrugged, his face a mix of embarrassment and joy.

"All right, then. Let's get started," Pastor Carter said as he shifted slightly toward Amanda to begin the vows. Because Amanda was more of a traditional gal, or had been, before her wedding had gone off the rails, she'd opted for more traditional vows. "Repeat after me," Pastor Carter said. "Sam, I promise to love and cherish you forever, to honor and support you, in sickness and in health, through hard times and good, and to be true to you every day of my life, until death do us part."

Amanda's voice wavered and broke as she repeated it, her eyes focused on Sam's. She wanted him to know just how much she meant it.

Afterward, Pastor Carter asked Sam to say the same thing, which he did in that kind and confident voice Amanda had fallen in love with. Pastor Cater then passed them the silly mood rings, which they slid onto one another's fingers.

"Now, let's see what color they turn into," Pastor Carter joked as the rings settled and adjusted to their temperatures. "Does anyone remember what color means they're in love?"

On Amanda's side of the aisle, Charlotte's daughter, Rachel, waved her hand and said, "Purple!"

Everyone laughed as Pastor Carter said, "Leave it to a teenager to tell us that, right?"

Amanda and Sam watched intently as their rings slowly transformed, bleeding from blue to green to yellow, before they both finally landed on purple. Amanda's smile shattered her face.

"We have purple, everyone!" Pastor Carter announced. "I'd now like to introduce you to Mr. Sam and Amanda Fuller. You may now kiss the bride!"

As Sam kissed her, there beneath the shimmering moon at the end of the most gorgeous day Martha's Vineyard had ever known, Amanda closed her eyes and allowed herself to fade into the romance of the moment, to forget every single heartache she'd ever experienced. Had you asked her at this moment if she'd ever been left at the altar, if Chris had ever hurt her so badly, she'd have said, "I don't know. Maybe in another life." Before them, their wedding guests roared with joy, then watched as Sam and Amanda paraded down the aisle as the string quintet played a peppy version of "This Will Be (An Everlasting Love)" before they collapsed between the double-wide doors and kissed some more.

They'd made it. They'd made it down the aisle. And now, the rest of their lives could begin.

Chapter Twenty Six

For the first time in what felt like days, weeks, or maybe even years, Kelli sat down. Xander had led her to the table where their name tags sat next to traditionally beautiful china, around which were three types of forks, three types of knives, a tiny spoon, an even tinier spoon, and two types of glasses. Kelli had known the dinner would be extravagant, but this was really something. Xander reappeared at the table with a glass of wine for her and a beer for himself, and he collapsed next to her and unbuttoned his suit jacket. "What a day," he said.

Kelli laughed and leaned into him, kissing his cheek and his lips.

"Hey, you two!" Claire appeared at the table with her husband, Russell, and bent to hug Kelli. "I can't believe you're not asleep right now."

"Trust me. Once I get through this meal, I'll be out like a light," Kelli said.

"You have to stay for a bit of the dancing," Claire urged her. "Besides. I heard you're out two different

A Vineyard Love

managers now. So, who will watch the hotel if you go home?"

Kelli waved a hand toward the back, where she'd asked one of her mid-grade managers, Calvin, to take over for the night. He'd already begun to order people around arrogantly in a way that indicated he couldn't have the role for long. But this ignited a memory, which led Kelli to text Officer Bobby immediately.

> KELLI: Hey. Is it possible Sandra framed Piper last week? Can you check in on that? I'd like to ask Piper back, if possible.
>
> OFFICER BOBBY: Sandra already admitted to it.
>
> OFFICER BOBBY: I have a few things to tell you based on what we learned.
>
> OFFICER BOBBY: I know you have a party up at the hotel right now, but do you mind if I stop by? I can come in plain clothes so that I don't freak out more of your guests.

Kelli showed the messages to Xander, who shrugged. "Might as well find out what he's talking about, I guess."

Kelli wrote back that Officer Bobby was welcome and that he could even have a plate of food if he wanted to.

> KELLI: You helped so much all week. I can't thank you enough.

As Charlotte, her fiancé, Everett, Andy, Beth, Steve, and Rina joined their table— all of Kelli's siblings and their dates or partners, Kelli smiled warmly, settling into the comforts of home. Before she totally forgot, however, she texted Piper with the news.

> KELLI: Piper, I am so sorry for the confusion. The cops have just learned you were framed. I don't know quite what to say. I hope we can work something out if you haven't already found another job. Let me know if you can come in tomorrow to discuss a potential hotel manager position (basically my job, I mean) with a hefty raise along with it. I hope we can work together far into the future.

Piper wrote back almost immediately.

> PIPER: The cop just called me. I'm so sorry about what you went through today! I'd love to meet you tomorrow. I'm just so relieved the chaos of this week is over...

Dinner was exquisite. Chef Billiard went all out with a five-course meal: an appetizer of crab cakes with a creamy sauce, a fresh salad with blue cheese, a sinful French onion soup, a steak cooked in pepper sauce, and a raspberry tart with rhubarb ice cream on the side for dessert. As they ate, Kelli, her siblings, and their partners (or Rina, who was just a friend) laughed and exchanged stories, scraping their plates clean. When Amanda and Sam approached their table to say hello, everyone insisted on taking selfies, pulling Amanda and Sam this way and that to smile and pose.

"My face is going to freeze like this!" Amanda joked to just Kelli.

After dinner, Amanda and Sam cut the wedding cake

and were ordered into the center of the room for their "first dance." The guests crowded around, craning to see more of the happy couple as they held one another and swayed gently to "You Are The Best Thing" by Ray LaMontagne. Just as Sam whirled Amanda around in a circle, his hands around her waist, Xander squeezed Kelli's upper arm gently and tilted his head toward the foyer. Officer Bobby had arrived, dressed in a pair of jeans and a button-down. He looked strangely uncomfortable out of his uniform.

Xander and Kelli walked quickly toward the foyer and led Officer Bobby to Kelli's office, thanking him for coming so quickly.

"You want anything to drink?" Kelli asked, surprised at how bright her tone was.

"Maybe after," Officer Bobby said. "It's been quite a day."

Officer Bobby sat in the chair across from Kelli's while Xander remained standing to Kelli's right, his arms crossed over his chest.

"So. I have some more information about the man and woman who robbed you today," Officer Bobby said. "And I don't think you're going to like it."

Kelli tilted her head. "I already don't like it, Bobby. What's up?"

Officer Bobby's cheek twitched. "Sandra Collings' fiancé and accomplice, Reggie Fitzgerald, just got out of prison about six months ago. When I learned that, I had a hunch about what prison he was in."

Xander placed his hand on Kelli's shoulder in recognition. It was obvious what would come next.

"It seems like Reggie and your ex-husband, Mike, got chummy on the inside," Officer Bobby said.

Kelli closed her eyes and allowed this information to fall over her like a crashing wave. How was it possible that Mike's hate could find her all the way outside of the thick walls of his prison, all the way to this hotel that he'd never even been to?

"Mike knew about your hotel endeavors and, it seems, about your new relationship with Xander Van Tress," Officer Bobby continued. "He made it clear to Reggie that he didn't care if Reggie shared any of the stuff he stole or any of the money he got out of it. He just wanted Reggie to ruin the hotel's grand opening."

Kelli was quiet for a long time, her head hazy from fatigue and disbelief. Finally, she heard herself say, "Wow." But it couldn't possibly encapsulate how she felt. She felt wronged. She felt alienated. She felt frightened, deeply frightened of Mike in a way she hadn't been since she'd left him.

"We've reported this news to the prison," Officer Bobby said. "And Mike will be appropriately punished as an accomplice to this robbery. But I wanted to pass along the news myself before all the mess of the trial starts up."

"Thank you, Bobby," Kelli managed as Xander's grip on her shoulder tightened, proof he was there for her; he was there to hold her up through this storm and whatever life threw at them next.

As Kelli, Xander, and Officer Bobby descended the staircase, approaching the ballroom once again, Amanda and Richard were out in the middle of the dance floor, dancing to the father of the bride song, "My Girl," by The Temptations. Kelli paused at this distance to watch them. Richard's eyes flooded with tears as Amanda said something to him, laughed, then began to cry, as well. It warmed Kelli's heart to see this. Three years ago, Richard had insulted Susan and wronged his children when he'd left. Yet now, because of the goodness of Amanda's heart, they could come together and celebrate new love— despite the mistakes of the past.

"You okay?" Xander asked, his face next to hers, gazing out across the historic ballroom.

"I'm just thinking," Kelli said.

"That's a dangerous thing, isn't it?" Xander joked.

Kelli laughed and placed her head on his shoulder, and he drew his arms around her waist. Officer Bobby waved and continued down the stairwell, headed for the bar to grab himself that drink. Kelli's heart swelled with love for this gorgeous place, which had nearly killed her, and the wonderful people who celebrated before her. She wasn't sure how she'd gotten so lucky.

"Look at them," Kelli said wistfully. "They're at the very beginning of all of life's adventures."

Xander kissed her cheek. His breath was hot as he said, "I have a feeling we are, too, my love."

Kelli twisted around to gaze at him. Her first instinct was to refute that, to remind him that she was in her late forties, that she wasn't getting any younger. But the youth and vitality reflected back in his eyes made her rethink that. What was age, anyway? It had nothing to do with her. If the world wanted to call them "old," it could do as it pleased. Xander and Kelli would have their fun, regardless— all the days of their lives.

Next in the Series

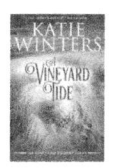

Pre Order A Vineyard Tide

Other Books by Katie Winters

The Vineyard Sunset Series

Secrets of Mackinac Island Series

Sisters of Edgartown Series

A Katama Bay Series

A Mount Desert Island Series

A Nantucket Sunset Series

The Coleman Series

Made in United States
North Haven, CT
02 January 2025